BEHIND A

BROKEN

SMILE

Black Shuck Books
www.blackshuckbooks.co.uk

First published in Great Britain in 2022 by
Black Shuck Books
Kent, UK

Versions of the following stories have previously appeared in print:
'Waxing' in *Suffer Little Children* (Black Shuck Books, 2019)
'The Deer' in *Voices* (Sinister Horror Company, 2021)
'A New Life' in *Shoot* (Green Ink Writers Gym, 2021)
'Along the Long Road' as a chapbook (Fox Spirit Books, 2018)
'The Farm' in *Dark Voices* (LVP Publications, 2018)
'Non-Standard Construction' in *Great British Horror: Dark Satanic Mills*
(Black Shuck Books, 2017)
'Origami' online at Ad Hoc Fiction (2015)
'Places to Run, Places to Hide' by the University of Leicester (2014)
'The Final Cut' in *Trickster's Treats 3: The Seven Deadly Sins*
(Things in the Well, 2019)
'To Pray at Your Temple' in *Dreamland: Other Stories*
(Black Shuck Books, 2021)
'The Lepidopterist in *Emerge* (Green Ink Writers Gym, 2020)
'Dendrochronology' in *The Woods* (Hersham Horror Books, 2019)
'On the Island' online at Jack Wallen: Dark Twisty Fiction (2021)

Set in Caslon
Titles set in Blanch
Cover art by James Worrad
Interior design © WHITEspace, 2022
www.white-space.uk

978-1-913038-79-3

Behind a Broken Smile

by

Penny Jones

BLACK
SHUCK
BOOKS

For Mrs Beasley,
a far better teacher than the one within these pages.

| Contents |

~

|Penny Jones|
by Robert Shearman

~

I enjoy not quite remembering how we first met. It was in Derby, at some writers' thing, that much I'm sure about. Was I a guest? Some rather minor guest? I think I was hosting a raffle, anyway. And as I went through the auditorium and up on to the stage, Penny Jones spoke to me. I spoke back. There may have been some banter. I don't know what. What I *do* know is, the next time I met Penny, she came up to me and apologised. She said she'd been very rude. And this I remember too – the expression on her face. Because the apology was real – but the face suggested that whatever it was she'd said, she still secretly thought it was pretty funny, and that she was pleased she said it. It's somewhat frustrating, I admit, that I can't recall the actual rudeness, but only how much pleasure it had given her.

Anyway, I refused to accept the apology. That would have been too easy. I said I was still very offended. She laughed, but I don't know she was entirely sure I was joking. And I laughed too, but I wasn't entirely sure what I was laughing about.

So our friendship began. There are worse ways.

Over the years I've realised that the best way to approach Penny's work is with a similar sense of ambiguous trepidation. That it *might* be funny – but that Penny won't necessarily want to tell you. Certainly I know that I'll start one of her stories with a smile on my face, enjoying the way she skewers her characters and puts them in distorted near-real worlds that verge on satire. But I always leave them a bit rattled. They're disturbing – and not just for the grisly subject matter, but for the somewhat mocking, somewhat aloof tone. Did I really just read what I thought I read? Was that actually what the story was about?

And, deep down – does Penny Jones really understand quite how deliciously odd she is?

As I say, I enjoy not really remembering the details of how we met. Because, like a Penny Jones story, there's no simple beginning to it. And without a proper start to our friendship, I sometimes feel that Penny has always been there – the kindest (and wickedest) of writers on the British horror circuit, the most supportive (and most ironic), the wisest (and by far the silliest). Her short, sharp tales are so compact and so complete that I can't be sure how I wandered into them. Most horror stories have doors – nice easy ways in, obvious exits out – and instead Penny drops you into rooms with high walls all the length around. I find them hard to read back to back, because for all their brevity, they feel heavy. Some writers tell stories that flow like water – easy to swallow, easy to forget. Penny's are like gravy, rich and thick, with bits bobbling about the surface that may or may not be meat. They're pieces of poetic prose that demand you to slow down, to consider the weight of each word. And to consider how you should react to those words – because they're also *funny*. No matter how dark the tale, there's an element of mockery to Penny's work, mocking the reader and mocking itself. These are stories that dare you to take them too seriously, for fear she'll show the absurdity beneath them. And that dare you not to take them seriously enough, for fear she'll show real pain and real anger and real dread.

We're good friends now – legitimately so, I feel. When she insults me now, she no longer feels the need for a follow-up apology. And I suppose I could ask her what really happened that first time we met in Derby. What on earth did she say? How on earth did I react? She might tell me. But I've no reason to believe what she might say. Like any good storyteller, Penny knows the value of telling truths, but not necessarily in a way that ever actually happened. So I won't ask. I shall continue to enjoy the ambiguous world of Penny Jones.

Welcome. I hope you enjoy it too.

—Robert Shearman
August 2022

|Waxing|

∿

"Would you like to keep it?"

I shake my head, my pigtails whipping sharp against my cheeks.

"But it looks a bit like you. Are you sure you don't want it?"

I turn the doll over and over in my hands, the golden hair turned straw by a thousand brushings, the dress probably blue originally to match the doll's eyes, now a faded grey from the grubby grasp and cradle of a hundred children's arms. The rag doll certainly does look a little like me. The only difference between the two of us is the bulge of stuffing that lies around its middle, stretching the worn material of the dress. I imagine the seams beneath puckered and splitting against the extra padding that lay inside.

"You can keep it you know, at least for tonight."

I place the doll on the desk and cross my arms; fighting the urge to flip the doll upside down to search for those seams, to see those criss-cross scars where someone had stuffed it, bloating it until the dress stretched against its body, the material tight, giving it curves that weren't there naturally. But the painted eyes of the woman watch me, study me still. Those eyes, rimmed black, would narrow as her hand reached out; elegant fingers, blood red and sharp at the tip would caress my skin. Instead, those fingers grasp the doll by the head and drop it on my lap once more.

"Don't you want her?"

Again I shake my head. I want to explain, to tell her how Father would be upset. That when I'd arrived at Hillcrest, Tammy – my own doll – had been taken away. That I was told on entering that I was too old for such toys, that frivolity was a weakness, that to play was a sign of idleness in children and madness in adults. A decadence that would not be tolerated within the house.

"All you need to do is show us…not what he did…just where he touched you."

I stand. I do not speak, I just allow the doll to drop to the floor.

~

The next day I awake with the sun, the quietness of my room disturbing my slumber. Here I'm on my own, no sound of breathing to lull me to sleep or cries in the night to shatter my dreams. On the first night they'd tried to close the curtains, hiding me away from the meagre light of the moon, shrouding me in the room's darkness. But each time they'd snuck in I'd woken, fighting them over the curtains, until finally the rail holding them snapped, the material hanging askew against the window, the plastic thrusting jaggedly like a snapped bone into the room. They removed the rail the same night, and so far no one had replaced it.

I roll over to face the window, to allow the weak sunshine to bathe my face in its warmth. My stomach drops as I turn. Someone had managed to sneak into my room during the night, as atop my bedside cabinet, the ragdoll slumps, blue eyes glinting in the early morning sun. Its head lolls down, as if it's staring at the mound of its bloated stomach. I try to ignore the fear that twists in my bowels as I get up, making sure to keep my face blank and my steps steady as I creep my way barefoot into the bathroom, wondering which one of them had snuck in with their gift whilst I slept.

I have no names for them, they all look the same to me, dressed in clothes which cut up between their legs and wrap around their chests like second skins, their faces painted like clowns. When I'd arrived they'd tried to get me to change. Cajoling me, telling me that they only wanted to wash my dress, that it was dirty from the journey, that they would give it me back once it was washed. But I'd grasped the material of my dress to my body and refused.

Now I wash myself carefully under my dress, in my tiny bathroom, not turning on the light. Making sure that my skin is clean and that I don't smell; that I don't give them any reason to insist on removing my dress and forcing me to put on their immodest clothes.

When I finally emerge, pink and shiny beneath the grey of my dress, breakfast has been placed next to the doll. Its stitched smile smirks as it waits to see if I'll eat today. Most days I don't. I'm pretty sure they're drugging me. Yesterday I caved and ate a fruit pot and drank a glass of water, praying it would be safe. They must have hidden something under the sweetness of the juice, something to deepen my sleep, allowing them to sneak in and place the doll on the table next to me – though whether as a taunt or a bribe, I don't know.

Picking up the tray I place it against the door, arranging it just so: spoon across the bowl of porridge, metal tumbler of fruit juice stacked atop it. My hands hover until I'm sure that it's balanced, before I make my way back to the bed. Grabbing the doll and scooting under the sheets with it. Father's warnings echoing in my head, reminding me of their false eyes and ears that are always there, hidden, spying, waiting to catch you out, to lead you astray. I'm pretty sure they can't see me under here. They'll know that I've got the doll, that they've piqued my interest with it. But they'll have no idea what I'm doing with it.

Hopefully when I get back to Father he'll be proud that I'm remembering all my lessons. That I'm putting into practice all that he taught me and following the rules. I'm proud of my alarm system too. Now they can't just sneak in and pull the sheets back whilst I'm not watching for them, not without me hearing them, anyway. Though maybe *proud* is the wrong word. Father always taught us that *God opposes the proud, but gives grace to the humble*, and I'm pretty sure he meant that pride was something bad.

I push the pride down deep inside me and flip the doll over in my hands. Running my fingers over the material, so unlike my old ragdoll's, the skin feels smooth under my fingers, cool and pliable, like the leather of my old ballet shoes. It holds none of the warmth of the old rough cotton dolls of my childhood. The dress – although made of the same material – is separate to the doll, not stitched to the skin. As if whoever made it expected its owner to dress and undress it. Maybe once, when new, it came with a whole host of outfits, ones that some lucky girl could change it into at her whim, but if so, it would have to have been before the doll was restuffed, the stomach distended to fill the dress completely. Under the skirt, a mark draws its way down the top of the doll's thigh, a purpling which bleeds out from under the tight bodice of the dress. My hand cups my hip as my fingers fan out to cover the birthmark that mars my own flesh. I ease the dress up, inch by inch, wriggling it as I slowly expose the doll's body. The blot could be innocent, nothing more than a careless child's spilt ink, tendrils of it leaching across from the doll's hip, rolling across its stomach before fading along its plump thighs. No one here could know, no one here had ever seen. They tried when I first arrived – tales about a doctor, someone who wanted to make sure I was well, that there was nothing wrong with me. I refused, gripping my dress tight between my legs, told them "I was fine, very well, thank-you very much."

Concentrating on the now-naked doll, I can see the myriad of marks, the inked moles and beauty spots, the stitched scars and puckered flesh. My fingers dance over my skin, as my eyes mark each imperfection on the doll's façade. My mind trips back to the fruit cup last night, the sweetness curling in my stomach, causing it to grumble in hunger.

"If you want to keep it, you must eat."

The doll is clamped under my arm; I no longer let it out of my sight. I even sleep with it under my pillow. I wonder how many girls before me they have tried to drive mad with it. The marks on the body made as I slept, the rips in the dress as I sat on the toilet, the yellow stains which have leached into the grey material, left there, I expect, from the minute strands of cotton they have threaded through the seams on the doll's armpits in my moments of distraction. *How could we manage such things.* Their statement becomes a question in my mind *How could they manage such things?* I've stopped brushing my teeth. The toothpaste is drugged as surely as the food they put on my plate. I heard you can go five weeks without food.

I hope that Father comes and gets me soon.

My head hurts. I've stopped drinking the water. I was stupid really not to realise. I thought I was so clever, sneaking drinks from the tap in my bathroom, rather than from the glasses that they poured me with my meals. It wasn't the similarities that caused me to see, to understand; it was the difference. There was only the one, and at first it was tiny, miniscule, a gradual change that would easily be missed by all but the most diligent.

Each morning I would sit in the chair by the window. There was no longer a need to hide beneath the sheets, they already knew that I was on to them. The element of surprise gone, I studied the doll in the bright morning sunshine. Stripping the doll of its dress no longer took minutes of careful prying and easing of material. The dress now slipped off with one sharp tug on the hem, the material flipping inside out as the collar sticks momentarily on the rag doll's head. I check the dress; the material, still stiff, hasn't ripped along the seams, and there are no visible signs of damage or wear to explain the ease with which the dress had come away. I'd put the preceding days' speed down to nothing more than that I was becoming more practiced at checking over the doll, my fingers more adept at stripping it back as I came to know each inch of its body. But maybe the answer isn't in my skill at all, but rather in the natural stretch of a material which had been done and undone a hundred times. I pull at the dress but there's no apparent give, no sign of thinning or sagging in its leather. I prod the stomach of the doll, my fingertip no longer finding the hard resistance, dipping the pink leather, the material wrinkling for a second before springing back fresh with no sign of my intruding finger having marred its flesh. I lift the doll to my eyes, the stitching on the seams still neat and tight, no sign of stuffing poking through. I try to cover up my discovery, to act normally as I go through the rest of my routine, checking the doll inch by inch, but it's no good. They will know, through their false eyes they will have seen all, and know that I have discovered their latest game.

"We need to set up a drip."

They think I can't hear, that I'm asleep. Even without their drugs I can't stay awake now. I'm exhausted. There's no longer any point in not eating or drinking, I'm so weak that I'm asleep more often than I'm awake. My skin now matches the leather of the doll in texture as well as tone. My hands pucker as they pluck at my flesh to insert the needle, the skin standing proud in ridges, as wrinkled as the now fully-deflated stomach of the doll that I hold against my own distended one. I rip the needle out, the tissue paper skin tears along the needle's length, the only act of defiance that I have left.

I want to roll over but my stomach won't allow it. I've watched it grow fat, even though I haven't eaten for weeks. I don't know how they did it, how they were drugging me. I wasn't eating, or drinking, I'd even stopped using the soap and shampoo in case the drugs were leaching into me that way. Maybe it was in the air, blown in through the air vents – I lash out as the women come closer, knocking the doll. It falls against the cotsides that encircle the bed; quickly my hand scoops it up, cradling it against my engorged chest before they can snatch it away – Yes, the air vents is the only explanation, or at least the only one that doesn't sound insane. It doesn't seem to matter now anyway. The knowledge that I did everything I could is the only thing keeping me going. I overheard one of the women talking about Father the other day, apparently he's been locked up. So there's no point hoping that he'll come and rescue me, not if there's no one to rescue him.

"You'll have to restrain her."

The women grab at my arms; leather straps, the same pink as the doll's flesh, encircle my wrists. Holding me down, they insert another needle into my hand. I watch as the tip punctures the vein that stands prominent as I grip at the doll, my fingers digging into its withered skin. I kick my legs, twisting, as they strap them into stirrups, raised, exposed. My dress puddles around my waist. The weight of my stomach pushing down, the doll is snatched away – limp, flaccid, an empty shroud – as my fingers curl, their nails cutting into my palms as I push against the pressure. I breathe, I push, I scream.

|The Deer|

The cars slow discordantly as the houses become ever distant from the road.

50, 40, 30.

Lorries speed past crowded terraces, shaking the windows and rattling the knockers of doors that open straight onto the mean, narrow pavement which houses a multitude of bins and recycling boxes that children weave themselves around. Their mothers brazenly ignore the revving engines and the blasts of air horns that elicit a cacophony of barks from behind greying net curtains, as they continue to push prams through the ditches that edge the winding street. Once past those houses, with their frontages painted the colour of clay by years of passing traffic, the speed drops to 40. The school backs away on the corner, protected by railings and walls, whether to keep the community protected within, or without, is up for debate in the local pub; as the patrons complain about the increase in traffic, both pedestrian and vehicular, and the pollution which both bring to the houses that lie beyond the school's walls, set back from the road by meagre strips of lawn edged with flowers. The men stand griping over their pints of beer about the daffodils and turf that have been ripped up by tiny hands and by the treads of tires.

Past these houses lie the playing fields. A clear patch of land which stretches out, merging at a tangle of brambles and nettles with the farmer's fields beyond. The morning mist rolls across the football pitch, mingling around the rusted climbing frames and swings with the smog from the road. Once past here the road straightens, stretching itself, ready for the escape from the claustrophobic village and its claustrophobic inhabitants. But there is no speedy escape as the limit drops to 30 past the huge houses, which look like doll houses down their long driveways, barely visible above the high fences and ornate gates that protect them from the road. If you sneak across the farmer's fields, you can catch a glimpse of them. Pillars that flank doorways, swimming pools that gleam invitingly, their waters forever still. Daffodils neatly planted and lawns deftly manicured, not a blade out of place.

The deer appeared to materialise from nowhere, a delicate spectre in the road. Rod slammed his brakes on as the shadow flitted through the mist that spread tendrils across the early morning road, the rising sun shining a corona of light that for a moment perfectly framed the image that printed itself across his windscreen. His tires slipped on the road, slick from the early morning frost. The impact forced him forwards, his belt cutting into his rotund, beer belly, expelling the stale smell of lager and whisky that had settled in his stomach from the previous night at the village pub. Shakily Rod stepped from the car, taking in short, sharp breaths of the frigid morning air, which burnt his throat like the previous night's whisky.

The front of the car had mercifully little damage. Rod ran his hands over the dented bumper as he cast his eyes around looking for the deer. The road was empty, save for a muddy shoe emblazoned with stars which one of the local kids had discarded, probably after standing in dog muck. Rod gingerly picked it up, sniffing at it before chucking it in the bin that stood next to the playing field's entrance, where a trail of melted frost led away from his car. Rod wiped his hand over his hair, realising too late about the mud or faeces that coated his fingers from the shoe; he was not thinking straight, he would have to calm down before he ended up panicking. He'd take the car back, shower and change before work – better to be a few minutes late than turning up smelling like something that had died in a ditch. Rod glanced at the dark line that trailed out from behind his car to the playing fields. Blood or faeces spattering the pitted tarmac along the way, a deadly spoor, marking the trail where the deer had dragged itself away to die. Sighing he headed over towards the playing field's entrance.

Halfway between the car park and the playground he found it. Head cocked at an odd angle, blood pooling beneath it, the deer lay crooked and broken upon the ground. Rod felt his stomach rise up into his throat as he headed over towards the body. It was smaller than he expected, maybe a fawn or a muntjac. The body gave slightly as he nudged it, testing the weight with the tip of his shoe, the suede turning darker, though whether from the melting frost that dripped from the grass or blood from the body he didn't know.

The sound of shouting echoed across the field from the adjacent house, the words muted by walls and windows, but the intention clear. *Hurry up*.

Rod gazed down into the glazed eye of the animal at his feet, even in the morning's icy temperatures a fly was already crawling around the edge of the socket, searching for an ingress. In the distance a magpie eyed him warily, but still inching closer, weighing up the risks posed to him against the rare winter food source.

The voice echoed again from the neighbouring house, part sentences terminated by the slamming of car doors ...*too late. Hurry up*.

Rod looked down in disgust at the corpse; he should move it, he couldn't leave it here for the council to clear up. Even if he phoned them now, they probably wouldn't pick the call up until they started work, so that'd be nine, then a cup of tea and sorting out rotas, etc. They probably wouldn't send anyone out until at least ten. Then it would take them a good half hour from the council offices in town to get all the way down here. God knows how many mothers with their toddlers would have wandered over to the playground after dropping the kids off at school by then.

He bent down, his gorge rising as his hands clasped the shit-covered legs, although better that then the lolling head with its vacant eyes staring up at him in reproach. He tugged. Nothing. He tugged again, and a ripping sound made his breakfast propel itself up his throat. He swallowed it down, telling himself that the noise was nothing more than frost as the cooling corpse froze against the too long winter's grass, though images of skin and flesh parting from bone sped through his mind.

He steeled himself, he only had to drag it across the football pitch and then he could hide it behind the equipment shed, out of sight until the park keeper could come and clear it up properly. Rod braced his feet and pulled at the corpse; it shifted a couple of inches. Digging in with his feet he tried to ignore the feel of bones disconnecting in the body's legs as he heaved it across the grass. Instead he focused on the gate, watching for the first sign of children making their way towards the school. Luckily, he thought, there wouldn't be too many of them having to pass by the field. If the school had been on the other side it was likely that the entrance to the field would already have been plugged with gawkers and rubber-neckers trying to see what was going on.

"Sam! Where the hell are you? I'm leaving now!"

The voice echoed from the house that bordered the field, the words distant but clear now. No walls or slamming doors to muffle the impatience obvious in their tone.

Rod looked behind him, making sure that he wasn't going to crash into the corner of the equipment shed. His heart dropped as he saw the distance, his arms felt like they'd been dragging the deer for miles, but the shed seemed almost as far away as it originally did. There was no way he'd get it there before the rest of the village made their way out of their houses. Rod looked at his car, his pride and joy, and back down at the deer at his feet. His brain calculated whether he could fit the body in the boot, whilst his mind argued that he'd ruin his car, that it'd be years before he could afford another E-Class.

"Sam! If I have to come and get you, there'll be trouble."

Rod dropped the legs of the legs of the deer and hurried over to the car.

It seemed to take ages to get the deer in the boot; the body stiff from rigor mortis wouldn't bend, and the boot of the car wasn't really geared towards carrying roadkill.

Carefully Rod got in, trying to minimise the mess on his upholstery. He just prayed if he got anything on it, the valet service would be able to get it back out again. Slowly Rod drove the car back across the playing fields. Keeping the revs low, he prayed that the tires wouldn't rip the grass up too much. Last thing he wanted was some busy body reporting him to the council for damaging the playing fields. He'd just about made it to the tarmac edge of the car park before the first of the park's visitors arrived. He had expected a mother with a toddler in tow, or a kid dragging their dog round to do its business before school started. But the woman who stood at the gates was on her own, hair a mess, no make-up, clothes rumpled and mismatched – he'd have a fit if he saw his wife out looking like that. Rod pointedly ignored the woman, who by now was screaming and gesturing wildly as she darted across the car park towards him. Drunk or on drugs, he thought to himself as he pushed down the locking mechanism on his car door, relieved to hear the comforting clunk echo from the others. He eased his foot down on the accelerator as he clung to the edge of the car park, giving the woman a wide berth, glad when she realised that there was no help or handout in the offing coming from him, and she twisted away, heading towards the swings and climbing frame that stood empty in the middle of the field.

Rod checked his rear view mirror as he indicated left towards home, rather than right which would lead him towards the town, and then onwards to work. Watching the woman run in jagged sprints across the field behind him, swerving from the swings to the shed, back to the slide, before veering towards the public loos. He hoped that Suzie would be out. He tried to remember if today was one of the days she worked, or went to the gym, or whatever it was she did once he left for work each day. He just wanted to get home, get showered, then get back out. Work were already going to be pissed that he was late; he didn't want to have to waste time explaining himself to his wife too.

Rod stripped in the boot room; stuffing his clothes into a plastic carrier bag, he tied the handles and propped it by the back door. He stunk, and although it was only a deer, he couldn't bear the idea of wearing those clothes again. No matter how many times they were washed he was sure they would always carry the faint sweet stink of blood, shit and death. Thankfully the drive had been empty when he got home, but Rod had no idea how long he had before his wife returned. He racked his mind to remember what she might have said this morning at breakfast, but he was pretty sure that other than a perfunctory goodbye, he hadn't spoken a single word to her.

Hurrying up the stairs. Rod rushed naked across the landing into the main bathroom. He didn't usually use this one, and his normal shower gel was sat in the shower cubicle of their ensuite. But the bathroom had been closer and to be fair the idea of washing the deer from him in the same shower he used every day made him feel queasy. Lathering himself, the bubblegum pink sweetness seemed to do little to wash the scent of death away, instead the sickly odour seemed to intensify it. Turning the shower as hot as it would go, Rod scrubbed at himself with the loofah until his skin turned red. The smell lingered, but there wasn't much he could do about that, other than douse himself in deodorant and aftershave to try and mask the cloying odour that clung to him.

Once dressed in clean clothes Rod felt better, until he opened the door to the boot room. The smell of blood and shit was overpowering in the enclosed space. Rod pushed the casement window open wide. He knew his wife would nag him about leaving the window open, but he was more concerned about the smell than he was about burglars breaking in today. Rod picked a cleaning wipe from the pack under the sink and used it to pick up the carrier bag of clothes with his thumb and fore finger, holding it out away from his body as far as possible. He'd chuck them into the tip on his way to work, and maybe find out what he needed to do to get the council to dispose of the body in his boot.

Rod took the stairs up to his office. He usually took the lift up to the sixth floor, but the smell in his car seemed to have permeated into his fresh suit by the time he got to the office car park, and the idea of being stuck in that enclosed space surrounded by the stench made him heave. Luckily he had his own space in the underground car park. So no fighting over the last space, or worrying about leaving his car out in the sun – although still January the sky was clear, and the sun beat down on the other cars in the car park – at least he didn't have to worry about the sun's rays heating up the body in the boot, creating an even more unbearable stench than was currently there.

He'd intended to drop the deer at the tip, but when he got there he saw a sign stating that the tip wasn't open on Wednesdays and

Thursdays, and that he could take any refuse across the county to the other tip that would be open. He'd debated about just dumping the body and the bin bag at the gates, but the flashing light of the security cameras dissuaded him from this plan of action. There was no way he could get over to the other tip, it was in completely the wrong direction. He glanced at the opening times; if he worked through lunch maybe he could sneak out early and get there before it shut tonight.

It was gone six and he'd got several missed calls on his phone by the time he was able to leave. His late arrival hadn't gone un-noticed and Rod didn't think his boss would be placated by his pointing out that it had never happened before. So after several extra piles of paperwork had been unceremoniously dumped on his desk, and several comments about the "odd odour in here" that Rod passed off to a problem with the heating system, he finally watched his boss leave the office and head down the street towards the train station on the corner.

The car stank. There was no getting away from it, the smell of blood and shit had been joined by a miasma of rotting flesh that had wormed its way deep into every crack and seam of the car. Rod was sure he could hear the distant hum of bluebottles, though how on earth they could have got into the car was beyond him. Starting the ignition, he allowed the purr of the engine to fill his ears, masking any sign of buzzing from the boot. He debated about cracking the window, but decided against it – it would probably do little to alleviate the smell, and his mind filled with the image of a thousand more bugs swarming in through the open window to feast on the rotten flash in the boot. The mere thought of the flyblown corpse in his boot when he finally got it to the tip tomorrow, maggots crawling from its eyes, made his skin crawl. Rod scratched at his arm as the material from his shirt played against his hairs as if a million tiny legs crept across his body, causing his skin to creep in response. Turning up the radio, Rod didn't hear his phone ringing in his briefcase.

"God you stink."

"Thanks love." Rod loosened his tie and slipped his shoes off.

"Go take a shower" His wife swerved round him, arms raised to avoid accidentally brushing against him. "I'll bring dinner back."

Rod made his way up the stairs, stripping as he went. He grimaced as he pulled his shirt off, the stench seemed as strong on him now as it had this morning. He just prayed that the garage would be able to get the smell out of his upholstery, or his car would be ruined. Balling his clothes up he stuffed them into the washing basket, suit and all, Susie would just have to sort them out tomorrow for the dry cleaner. He was just turning on the shower when he heard the sound of the garage door opening below, the *clank, clank, clank* of the door rolling up echoed oddly through the ensuite's floor. It was one of the plus sides of the house that the master bedroom was situated over the garage, meaning that even if people were up and about downstairs you couldn't hear them up here. Rod turned up the heat on the shower, and stepped in. As he heard the bleep from his key fob, Rod realised why the sound was so out of place in the usually quiet room. It was because only he parked his car in the garage. Susie always parked on the drive at the side of the house – worried that she'd either scratch her car or, worse, his.

Rod threw open the shower door and ran, feet slipping on the tiled floor, over to the window and pushed it open. "Susie!" There was no answer, just the sound of the car engine running. "Susie!" Throwing a towel round his waist Rod thundered down the stairs. The door stood open in the boot room, the wind funnelling through from the open garage door, whipping the towel round Rod's legs. He clasped it between his thighs, suddenly aware of his nakedness. Susie stood in the doorway clutching something in her hands.

"I left you a message." Her fingers tightened, twisting on the object held before her.

"Susie. Don't. My car. I can explain…"

"I said I needed to use it. Mine's in the garage, and I need to pop to the shops. Just to get some bits. For Debby. She's had a bit of a shock."

"…I hit a deer. I didn't want to leave it for anyone to find. The smell…" Rod shuffled towards Susie, gripping the towel in one hand, he raised his other in an attempt to calm her. As she flinched away, he noticed the open boot. "Susie?"

"Her son's missing; they've been searching all day. The police have told her to stay in, in case he comes home. She's got no food in. I was just going to pop to the shops."

"Susie. Honey. It's fine. I'll go. I'll throw my clothes back on and have another shower when I get back. Just take some deep breaths." Rod reached out in an awkward embrace, dropping the towel by accident as Susie stepped back towards the threshold. "It's okay love. It's only a deer."

Tears spilled from Susie's eyes as they darted between her husband and the garage, her breath hitching, her hands rhythmically twisting the object held within them to and fro.

"Here calm down, it's okay, have a seat. Why don't you give me that?"

Susie yanked her hands away.

"It's only a deer. I'll take it to the tip tomorrow, get it properly disposed of." Tears flooded from Susie's eyes as she finally dropped the item she was holding to the floor. It blended in seamlessly, the tiny shoe, amongst their trainers and boots. The dark patches on it could have been anything: mud, blood, dog shit. There was no way to tell, but even through the reddish-brown stains Rod recognised the stars that peeked through.

|A New Life|

~

The new lawn lay square and neat, each blade of grass cut the same, lying down in straight, even rows. A woven blanket of green hiding the ground beneath. Even Peter couldn't have found fault, there wasn't a stem out of place.

Sarah stared at her handiwork. Gone were Peter's rose bushes, that twisted mess of thorns that he tended to so carefully. It wasn't as if she had been jealous of the roses. Sure he showed them a tenderness that was sadly lacking towards her, but any moment of time he lavished on them was one that she didn't have to endure. She'd watch him snipping away as their blooms wilted and faded. *Although it appeared harsh*, he would tell her, *it's what was best for them*. Peter always knew what was best.

Sarah slipped off her too tight court shoes. Muddy and scratched, she should have found something more suitable, but the garden had never been her domain. Peter hadn't even trusted her to water his plants. But Peter was gone, and someone would have to tend his garden... *her* garden now.

Sarah placed her stockinged foot upon the dew wet grass, hesitant for a moment as she waited for the expectant admonition. With a smile she pressed her foot against the lawn, her stocking soaking up the dew as it pressed the blades flat beneath her sole. She stepped forward, her feet joining each other on the soft turf. The ground springing beneath her as she twisted and turned, dancing to nothing but the beat of her heart and birdsong.

Her stockings were torn and laddered, her feet stained green from sap when she finally dropped to the ground. The neat lines of the lawn now twisted and scuffed. Divots and hills carved by her pirouettes dug into her bruised and aching muscles. Sarah lay there, allowing the peace and tranquillity to envelope her. "I will lie here all year. Bathe in the spring dew, bake in the summer sun, bury myself beneath the autumn leaves, to bud once more beneath the winter snow."

Sarah spread her fingers wide as she entwined them with the grass, the blades tickling at her skin, as she lay and listened to the sounds of the garden, the birds in the trees, the somnolent hum of the first questing honey bees. Even the ground beneath her seemed alive with sound. The scratch of the woodlouse as it wound its way around her body, trying to navigate its way home past this unusual obstacle that lay in its path. Sarah turned her head to try and see it as she felt its gentle touch traverse her body. Her skin prickled at its passage, but there was no sign of it. Beneath her ear she could hear the sound of earthworms and beetles and a myriad carrion insects as they burrowed their way under her, safe and warm within the nutrient rich soil below. The tickling on her skin was joined by another, then another. Her body suddenly besieged by bugs, her skin crawling, itching and burning beneath their delicate touch. Jolting upright, Sarah felt the grass pulling at her, heard the sound of ripping, though whether of her clothes or the grass she was unsure. She swept at her body, wincing as her hands caught at the fading bruises that still tattooed her skin. A sunset of yellow and purple, fading away to be hidden beneath her green sap-dyed skin.

Sarah stood staring at the patch of lawn. No longer neat and orderly, it looked wild and unkempt. A square of wild meadow ripped up and dumped unceremoniously within the neat suburban garden. The shape of her body lay imprinted on the turf, as if a ghost lay out there sunbathing in the weak evening light. Shuddering at the thought, Sarah closed the kitchen door and locked it, double checking the handle, before stripping off her ruined stockings and leaving then on the doormat. Her feet left muddy prints as she made her way through to the bathroom to shower the grass and mud from her body.

Bone weary, she left her filthy clothes in a pile on the bathroom floor and allowed the water to sluice away the dirt from her body, before wrapping herself in a towel and dragging herself to bed, the sky still painted crimson as the sun dipped behind the horizon. She knew she should have cleaned the floors: picked up her clothes and mopped up her muddy footprints. She would never have dared to be so slovenly if Peter was still here. But he wasn't, and her day of gardening had tired her more than she thought possible. For once she climbed into the bed without fear of repercussion.

It was already light when Sarah woke. The sun streaming through the curtains framed her in its light upon the bed. The house was quiet. For the first time since she could remember she wasn't woken by the sound of the radio, turned up high, as Peter sat in the kitchen waiting for his breakfast. She'd once loved to hear the radio in the morning, her grandfather listening to *The Archers* on a Sunday, her mum singing along to the pop hits as she'd packed Sarah's lunch for school. That had changed though since Peter. Now, rather than enjoying the radio, she used it as a barometer. It's volume warning her of the pressure that was building within, ready to erupt as she stepped gingerly into the kitchen each morning. This morning it was silent as she stepped into her slippers and made her way downstairs.

The mess was worse than she remembered. Mud had crusted on each stair, the carpet matted with sap and dirt that crumbled beneath her step. "It'll vacuum," she said to herself, grateful that at least this mess wouldn't take as much cleaning as the last one.

Sarah made her way into the kitchen, stepping around her muddy footprints as if dancing with herself, sidestepping her mess whilst she made breakfast. Sarah popped two slices of bread in the toaster as she waited for the kettle to boil. She caught sight of her stockings lying coiled in a pile on the mat. A moulting just lying there, as if yesterday she had simply shed her skin, shucking off her past and discarding it in one deft movement. Sarah reached out towards them, frayed and ruined; she wanted to hide them, to bury them beneath the rubbish in the bin, stuff them down deep amongst the rotting food and waste, throw them out and dance bare-legged forever more. The toast popped. The noise, loud in the quiet of her home, broke through the cacophony in her mind, shocking her as she dropped the stockings at her feet. Embarrassed she grabbed them, stuffing them away at the bottom of the bin beneath the remnants of the last meal she'd cooked for Peter. Carefully Sarah washed her hands, ensuring every inch was scrupulously clean before she buttered her toast.

～

The lawn looked a mess today, no longer square and neat. The grass, rather than the lush green of yesterday's freshly laid turf was instead either straggly or stunted, dependent where on the plot it lay. The shape of her body was still crushed into the centre of the lawn. An echo of things past, imprinted on the garden. The edges of the lawn crept across the patio, long tendrils reaching towards the house. The borders that she'd cut so carefully yesterday, slicing by hand with an edging knife, paring away anything that was superfluous, now twisted and twined. Fronds of grass wrapped themselves round the delicate flowers in their beds, dragging them down to the earth below.

The grass where she'd laid yesterday appeared dead, shrivelled and brown like hay. Sarah touched it with her fingers. The blight seemed to spread much further than where she lay, the shape on the ground a good six feet long, rather than her petite five foot frame. Sarah made her way to the shed. Searching through it she found an ancient tub of grass seed. Not wanting to make the patch any worse, she tiptoed round the edge of the figure, generously pouring the seed across the blighted grass. Filling the watering can from the water butt she sprinkled the seed, hoping that it was the right thing to do and she wouldn't just end up with a boggy mess for a garden. A sharp pain twisted in her ankle as she turned to put the can back next to the butt. Her shoe stuck in place as her body turned, spraining her ankle and toppling her to her knees. Sarah pulled her foot away hoping that the mud that sucked at her shoe hadn't seeped beneath her. The last thing she wanted to do was to mop the kitchen floor for the third time in as many days, because she'd tracked mud in once more. But the ground was dry, the grass crisp beneath her fingers as she wrenched her shoe from its tendrils.

～

Sarah watched as the birds pecked at the lawn. Blackbirds, crows, magpies, wrens and starlings. A shadow of birds blanketed the ground as they pecked at the seed. Digging and scratching, they pulled worms and insects from the freshly watered earth, turning it over to search for more food for their feast. She debated going out there and shooing them off, but there was no point; as soon as she came back in, they'd return. Better to leave them to it and assess the damage in the morning when they would hopefully have found pastures new to feed on.

Sarah pulled the curtains closed and tried to ignore the cacophony of song and calls and screeching in the back garden.

The next morning Sarah couldn't see the figure in the lawn. The grass around the edge had continued to steal its way towards the house, but the blades behind it – now equally as long – stood tall like sentinels.

The sound of birdsong was loud even through the closed windows, though Sarah could no longer see a single bird within the garden. Sarah watched as a light drizzle pattered against the window, the droplets gleaming in the sunlight. If she searched there would be a rainbow, arching high somewhere above her house. But instead she turned away, and headed further into her home, excusing herself from investigating the devastation left by the birds until the rain had stopped.

Sarah had avoided looking out of the window. She told herself there was no point, the weather was vile, and the rain made everything look grey and miserable. For three days she'd told herself this. Excusing her reluctance to set foot outside by the fact that it was raining, or it had rained, or it was about to rain once more. Today though the sun was bright. Even before she drew the curtains back, Sarah knew that the sky would be blue; washed clean, without a cloud. She tried to persuade herself otherwise, to keep the curtains shut tight against the inclement weather outside. But it was no use lying to herself, she would have to face it sooner or later.

Pulling back the bedroom curtains Sarah stared down in disbelief at her garden. Whether it was the seed, or the rain, or the earth, the grass had shot up. The patio was now completely hidden beneath a sea of green, its waves rolling in the breeze that tried to shake the tree branches free from the entangling fronds. A tendril of green twisted in the air in front of the bedroom window, back and forth in the wind as if watching her. More grass plaited itself round the drainpipe, climbing the house like ivy.

From below came the sound of tapping on a window. Sarah froze, sure that the tapping was the sound of the grass searching for an entrance, questing for a way into her home. The sound came once more and her fear bubbled over, threatening to turn to hysteria as she realised the sound came from the front of her house. Panicking that she was too late, that the grass had crept round the perimeter and surrounded her, trapped her within her own house, intent on burying her beneath itself… Relief flooded through her as she heard the voice shout out, although the words only momentarily alleviated her fear. "Mrs Harris. Please could you open the door. It's the police. We know you're in there. We need to speak to you about your husband." The tapping turned into a hammering. "Mrs Harris. We have a search warrant."

Sarah shot down the stairs, at the bottom she stared along the hallway. To the front lay certain danger; to the rear one unknown. In the end it was the anger – so like Peter's – in the policeman's voice that made her decision for her.

Sarah bolted for the back door. Throwing it open she took a step into the overgrowth, losing herself within the wilderness that grew there, hidden in her little patch of suburbia.

It seemed an age before she came to the clearing. Forcing her way through the grass as it pushed her this way and that. Guiding her or hiding her she neither knew, nor no longer cared. She allowed her body to succumb to the shoots that twined round her limbs. Each one dragging her, pulling her, coaxing her to lie down once more upon the barren figure that lay at the heart of the garden.

|Along the Long Road|

~

'Come on, it'll be fun.' Sienna pouted as she perched on the desk, flicking through a stack of letters as a front for why she was really there. 'Don't make me go on my own, it'll be boring.'

'I thought you said it would be fun.'

'See, I knew you'd come round.'

Beth rolled her eyes, safe in the knowledge that even if Sienna hadn't been scrolling through her Facebook feed, she still wouldn't have noticed the look, or the sarcasm in Beth's voice.

'And Adam'll be there, and you're the only one of my friends that he likes, he says that all the rest of them are airheads.'

'Ladies. Come on now less chit-chat, break times over, back to work.'

'Of course Mr Symonds, I was just helping Beth here with her letters.' Sienna fanned herself with the sheaf of envelopes in her hand, shifting imperceptibly, so that she was facing the boss, the front of her shirt settling against her breast.

'Well that's… that's very nice of you Sienna. I'm sure that Brenda…'

'Beth.'

'…Yes of course, Beth, is very grateful for anything you can do for her.'

Sienna smiled as she watched him walk back to his desk, rearranging his trousers as he sat down and glanced back over at her. Sienna winked at him; he ignored her, his face red as he buried himself in a pile of paperwork. 'As I was saying. Adam'll be there. I'm so lucky that my boyfriend and my bestie get on so well together. Well I'd better get back to work. See you tonight.'

Beth picked up the scattered envelopes and tried to put the correspondence back in some semblance of order. She'd bitten her tongue; of course she got on so well with Adam, she'd known him longer than he'd known Sienna. He'd gone out with her best friend Carly for years, that was before Carly had gone to uni and they'd drifted apart. She still saw Carly – mainly at Christmas when she came back to see her parents – but it wasn't the same between the two of them either. Carly never said anything, but her eyes were contemptuous when she spoke about her life: uni, work, friends, partners – both men and women – and her gaze would dull as soon as Beth spoke; keeping her updated on everything that had happened since she'd been gone – which mainly consisted of who'd married whom from school, and who they were now cheating on them with. Sometimes Beth thought that Carly seemed to think she'd seen and done everything, that she'd upped sticks and gone to uni somewhere glamorous like London or New York, rather than to the old technical college in Birmingham.

Beth eased the door to behind her. Stepping out of her shoes, she tip-toed down the hall, taking her weight on the banister, the stair creaking beneath her foot.

'Elizabeth where are you going?' the querulous voice, carried through the silence of the house.

'Nowhere Mum. I'm just back from work.'

'Work? Do you mean school? It's a bit late for them letting you out isn't it? Were you in detention again?'

'No Mum.' Tears pricked at Beth's eyes. She wasn't sure if the denial was in response to her mum thinking she was still at school, or to her query about her being kept behind in detention.

'Why don't you come in here and tell your old mum about it, before I make the tea.'

'I'll be in in a bit Mum. I need to go and have a shower.'

'Surely you can come and say hello first. Don't you want to spend some time with your dear old mum?' A deep sonorous chuckle emitted from behind the closed door, broken by a series of rasping coughs.

Beth held her breath, one foot on the stairs and one in the hallway, as she waited for either the coughing to subside, or for the choking to begin again. 'I'll be in in a moment Mum.' Crossing her fingers against the lie, Beth shouted over the coughing, 'It was P.E. today.'

As the sounds of coughing eased, and quiet once more descended on the house, Beth crept upstairs.

Beth yanked the brush through her unruly hair. They were out of conditioner again, she'd been pretty sure that she'd picked some up last time she went to the supermarket, but the bottle was empty – maybe she was getting as forgetful as her mother. It must be the answer, there were only the two of them; her dad had left when she was little, and although he'd kept in contact for a while – mainly it seemed, to tell Beth about how much of a harridan her mum was – he hadn't been interested once her mum had gotten ill, and Beth didn't want to push it too much in case he made her go and live with him. Though whether he could still do that now that she was technically an adult she didn't know – he certainly was no longer paying her mum any child maintenance, cause she dealt with all the finances these days, and those payments had stopped the day she'd finished sixth-form. And it certainly wasn't her mum using up all the conditioner, she couldn't even get to the downstairs loo without Beth helping her stand from her chair, let alone walk upstairs anymore.

Tears sprang to Beth's eyes as the brush pulled at her damp hair, its bristles caught in a knot. She gave up and allowed the brush to hang from her wet and tangled tresses, as tears slid down her face.

'Who are you?' Drool dribbled down her mother's chin as she watched Beth place the tray on the adjustable table at the side of her. 'Careful, that's an antique you know, a wedding present, precious in more ways than you could imagine. You'll scratch it.'

Beth pressed her fingertips against the scratched Formica surface of the bog-standard hospital table that the district nurses had brought round, and closed her eyes, counting slowly to herself until the frustration passed enough for her to speak calmly, without shouting at her mum. 'I'll be careful, I always am.'

'Who are you? What are you doing here?'

'Mum, it's me, Beth.'

'Beth?' her mum's eyes glared suspiciously at her 'My Beth? Elizabeth?'

'Yes Mum.'

'You're looking very grown up. Have you done something to your hair?'

'Here, have some of this before it goes cold. I've got to pop out in a bit, and I want to make sure you've eaten.' Beth pressed the spoon against her mum's shut lips, steam rising from the soup. Finally her mum opened her mouth, a red welt marring her skin where the spoon had been held, as if she had been putting on lipstick. She clamped her mouth shut tightly again and wrenched her head away, just as Beth had done when she was a toddler and her mum tried to make her eat sprouts.

'I won't eat it. It's too hot.'

Beth tapped the spoon against the back of her hand, the metal searing against her skin;she placed the bowl back on the tray. 'I'll try again later, when it's a bit cooler.' Beth stood and turned on the television; two people stood arguing, one of the soaps that her mum used to love so much. 'I'm just popping out for a bit Mum. See you later.'

Her mum's head swivelled towards Beth, but her eyes remained fixed on the television screen as she spoke. 'Well don't be late love, you've got school tomorrow.'

Beth ran down the road to Sienna's house, where Sienna was perched on the garden wall. Spying Beth turn the corner, Sienna draped her arm round Adam and pulled him towards her, pressing her lips against his and not breaking contact until Beth arrived.

'You know Adam could have come and picked you up from your house, then you wouldn't have had to run.' Sienna wrinkled her nose. 'Then you wouldn't have been so sweaty, and you could have worn some nicer shoes.' She held her arms out for Adam to lift her down, landing nimbly on a pair of heels so high she could easily have reached the ground from the wall on her own anyway. 'Now that you're here, someone's excited to see you.'

Beth looked at Adam, but he was studiously ignoring her, concentrating on buffing an invisible mark away on the wing of his car. Beth looked back at Sienna.

'No not me silly.' Sienna held her phone up, using her camera to check her hair, 'And not Adam either.' Her tone darkened as she spoke, her words stilted. 'Thought you might be fed up of playing gooseberry with the two of us, so I invited someone along, a double date.'

Beth scanned the street, but it was empty except for the three of them, 'I don't know, I mean if you wanted to be alone you should have just said.' Beth's voice carried in the somnolent, summer street. She glanced across at Adam, her eyes pleading, but he didn't even look her way, just opened the car door and sat himself in the driver's seat, the engine growling, music erupting from the stereo. In the distance someone tutted loudly, before slamming a window.

'Come on, it'll be fun.'

Beth wondered if Sienna really thought it would be fun; she said it a lot. In fact, it was the first thing she'd ever said to Beth. The first day that Sienna had started working at Symonds Retail she'd glanced around at the middle-aged women in their frumpy twinsets, shimmied past the old boys club in their hand made suits – which Beth presumed had once fitted them, and now fitted them slightly too well; the material shiny, matching the sheen of sweat across their brows – and made a beeline for the only other person in the office even close to her age. When on their lunch break Beth told her about whose wandering hands to avoid at the photocopier – pretty much everyone's – and who to avoid gossiping with over the kettle – Janice from accounts – and that other than that the job was pretty tedious, but at least it paid the bills. Sienna had smiled and replied that it didn't sound boring, it sounded fun.

Later Sienna made her way out of the kitchen, carrying two steaming cups of coffee across to Beth's desk. As she sat sipping her coffee Sienna smiled as Janice from accounts walked past carrying a box of doughnuts, and offered one to Sienna. 'Oh I shouldn't, I only have to look at one of these, and the pounds just pile on.' Sienna took the proffered doughnut though, winking at Beth, as Janice continued to offer the doughnuts to the rest of the office, ignoring Beth. 'I think

I'll like it here, everyone's so much fun.' Sienna said before taking a bite of her doughnut.

Everything was great fun to Sienna. That they worked together – though Beth wasn't quite sure what Sienna actually did, but she must have been good at it, whatever it was, as she'd been promoted twice since she'd started. That Beth and Adam knew each other – of course they did, Beth had been the one to introduce them, sort of. They'd been down the local after work when Adam had walked in. She'd been watching him for a couple of hours, trying to work out if she should go over and talk to him, now that he and Carly had split up, unsure if he'd even want to speak to her, now that he was no longer dating her best friend.

'Who you looking at?' Sienna had plonked two glasses of wine on the table, and was looking over her shoulder, back at the packed bar, to see who had caught Beth's eye.

'Oh no one, just someone I used to know, from school.'

Sienna had thrown back her wine, and insisted on getting another drink in; ignoring the pleas from Beth about it being her round, explaining that she'd just got her pay review and it was her treat. Beth had sipped at her glass of wine, and thought about the meagre money she had left at the end of the week, once the bills were all paid, and let Sienna go up to the bar. It wasn't until Beth had drained the entire glass that she realised that the wine had gone straight to her bladder; she looked up to see what was taking Sienna so long, not wanting to lose the table in the crowded pub. By the bar, Sienna stood in the centre of a group of males, laughing as she grabbed one of their phones, her nimble fingers, deftly typing something into it before she handed it back, to Adam.

Sienna opened the passenger door of the car and slipped in. Beth's fingers grazed the back door handle, voices mumbled from within but were lost in the heavy bass of the drums, which reverberated from the stereo system. The windows, tinted, showed the outline of someone already sat in the back seat.

'Come on slow poke.' Sienna's voice drilled through Beth's mind as the door pressed against her, bending her fingers back; whoever it was waiting for her in the back of the car pushed the door open impatiently.

'Do you remember Rob?' Sienna indicated at the balding hulk of a man who sat sweating in the cramped back seat of the car. 'I think you two were at school together.'

Beth slid into the car, nodding at Rob; his face, unfamiliar, seemed old. 'I don't think I do.' Beth pulled the door shut and sidled up as close to it as she could, before clicking her seat belt in to lock. Beth's skin crawled as Rob's gaze crept over her face and down her neck to her chest and body, lingering – she quickly removed her hands from the seat belt and held them clasped on her lap – before his gaze snapped to Sienna in the front of the car, next to Adam.

'I think Beth might be a bit younger than me Sienna.'

'Oh. Well she's not as young as me, so don't worry.' Sienna caught my eye in the review mirror and winked. 'You won't be cradle snatching.'

Beth wished that Adam's car had one of those arm rests that you could pull down onto the middle seat. Her dad's car had had one when she was little, and she'd always wanted to have a little brother or sister, so she could use it as a table to play games on during long drives. She'd mentioned this to her mum once, and her mum had smacked her – the only time – before bursting into tears. Her dad had left soon after, taking the car with the armrest table with him. Beth learned to not ask for anything after that.

'When did you leave?' Rob leant across the seat, closing the miniscule gap between the two of them.

'Huh?' Beth wasn't sure what he meant; she hadn't left, it had been her dad who left. She'd stayed, she'd had to.

'School. When did you leave? I left in 2000.'

God! He was thirty-five, and that was if he'd stayed on to do A-Levels. Did they even *do* A-Levels back then.

'2015.' Beth stuttered as she watched Rob pull away and lean forwards to speak to Sienna.

'I thought you said she was my age.'

Sienna just shrugged. Rob looked across at Beth and echoed Sienna's shrug, before settling back down, the gap closing, Beth felt the hard tip of the door handle press into her side.

'Where are we going?' Beth watched as the cinema flew by. They'd already headed out of town, away from the bars and the nightclubs, and now the leisure park was nothing but a distant memory in the review mirror, the bright lights of its restaurants and cinema fading into the twilight sky.

'It's a surprise.' Sienna twisted round to smile at Beth, 'I hope you all like surprises.' She winked at Rob before facing forwards once more, her hand reaching over and squeezing Adam's thigh once, firmly.

Beth realised that she was staring at Sienna's hand as it lay high up on Adam's leg. Sienna would only have to stretch her pinkie finger to stroke his groin. Beth's eyes strayed before she could catch herself; glancing up she saw that Adam was still concentrating on driving and Sienna was now ignoring everyone and pouting at her phone once more. The only person who watched her was Rob.

'Where are we?' The car cruised to a stop in a lay-by – well Beth presumed it was a lay-by but it didn't look much like one. In fact it didn't look like anything other than a patch of tarmac where cars had been forced to steal across onto the adjoining moorland, because they had encountered something approaching them along the narrow, rutted, mean road from the other direction. Mud splattered against Beth's window as Adam manoeuvred the car as far across the narrow space as was possible, branches scratched against the window, a thorn sharp and black lay next to her eye, Beth was glad that Adam's car had air conditioning, meaning she'd kept the window closed against the night's heat.

'I thought we would do something free as well as fun tonight.' Sienna had removed her seat belt and twisted round in her seat, her hands resting on the headrest, her eyes flicking to Beth. 'As you're always complaining about how much everything costs.' Sienna's gaze passed to Rob as she smirked 'I can't help liking the finer things in life, can I? Though they do say that the best things in life are free.' Sienna winked at Rob before she reached over and grabbed at Adam's shirt, pulling him in for a kiss.

Beth tried to ignore the grappling and the mutters of lust which emanated from the front of the car. There wasn't even any point in looking out of the window, as all that was framed there were the darkening, twisted boughs of the hedge which edged this part of the narrow lane. She felt something against her hand, and glanced down, Rob had inched his fingers across the miniscule gap between them on the back seat. Beth looked up and Rob indicated with his head to the couple in the front seat and shrugged, as if he too was embarrassed, but then he reached across and enclosed her fingers in his hot and sweaty palm. Beth yanked her hand away and placed it in her lap, turning once more to stare at the crawling brambles on her side of the car. She'd never felt so trapped before – even at home she could leave whenever she wanted to; even if she didn't, it was her choice – but here if she wanted to get out she'd have to climb over Rob, and the thought made her gag. She wasn't sure if he would even move to let her by if she asked, or if he would enjoy the sensation of her clambering over him.

She should feel safe here, she was amongst friends – well, at least two of the car's occupants were supposed to be her friends. Even if she didn't know Rob, she knew Sienna and Adam… surely they'd help her if she needed it, they wouldn't let Rob do anything that she didn't want to do.

'For God's sake Beth. Lighten up will you.'

Sienna's voice broke through Beth's thoughts, and she realised that she was sitting ramrod straight in the backseat, her eyes staring wildly as her mind tried to figure out a way to escape.

'This was supposed to be fun. But it's no fun if it's just the two of us, and you staring at us. I wanted to rough it a bit, but I'm not in to dogging or any of that pervy stuff.' Sienna squeezed Adam's thigh again. 'Why don't you two go for a walk or *something*?' Sienna winked again at Rob as she spoke the word 'something'. 'You know, give us two lovebirds some alone time. We don't need long, maybe half an hour or so.'

Rob smiled and opened the door, and the heat of the night swept through the car, obliterating the coolness of the air conditioning He stood in the doorway, one hand resting on the car door, the other extended towards Beth in a gesture of perfect gentlemanly behaviour to assist her getting out of the car, although, she thought to herself, surely it would have been more of the gentlemanly thing to get out of her way so she wouldn't have to inch past him. Beth ignored his outstretched palm and shifted across the seat. As she eased herself past him, the door frame dug sharply into her back, but she didn't allow even an utterance of discomfort to pass her lips, in case, in the confines of the space, it was misconstrued as a gasp of something else. Once she was out of the car, Beth made for the open road, taking deep breaths of fresh air as the warm, summer breeze embraced her. It was a lazy wind, as her mother used to call them – it didn't want to go round her, it wanted to go through her – but tonight that was fine, the coolness of the wind juxtaposed with the warmth of the night felt clean against her skin, and she shivered more against the wind's caress than the temperature.

'You cold?' Rob stood behind her. She hadn't heard him, his footsteps were very quiet, even over the gravel and detritus that was scattered over the edge of the road. 'Here, you can wear this if you want?' He held out his jacket towards her, but Beth just shook her head, and searched each way up and down the road. How long had it taken them to get here? Ten, maybe twenty minutes. How many miles was that? Could she walk it? Even if she did, what time would she get home? Her mum would be waiting, sat in the chair, bedsores forming, as the nurses told her they would if she gave in to her mum's demands: that she didn't want to go to bed, that she didn't *like* the new bed, that the rails reminded her of a cot, that she wasn't a baby. Screaming at her while Beth pulled the sides up, trying to avoid her mum's flailing arms and her sharp, filthy nails – they never seemed to be clean, no matter how much or how often Beth scrubbed at them.

Beth looked along the road in the other direction. The only sign of habitation was a distant stone cottage, too far for her to even be able to tell if there was a light on, or a car in the driveway. Though closer, that was still miles away, and she might get there and discover that the owner wasn't even in. Beth pulled her phone out of her pocket, but the bars at the top were conspicuous by their absence. Mobile phones had been around for years, you'd think by now they'd have sorted out the coverage, but there was nothing. Maybe if she was lucky she'd manage to send a text message, but she was pretty sure that taxi firms didn't respond to text messages. It was a good job she wasn't in trouble, cause God knows how she'd manage to call 999 out here. She shivered again, and Rob draped his coat round her shoulders.

'Come on, let's give those lovebirds a bit of privacy shall we.'

～

Beth trekked back across the moorland towards the car. Sienna might not have liked her shoes, but Beth was glad that she was wearing her trainers now instead of hooker heels like Sienna's. It hadn't taken Rob long to shed his gentlemanly front; they'd only walked a short way across the sparse scrubland before Rob had spotted a bench surrounded by a small copse of trees, their heavy foliage effectively screening the spot from the road. Rob sat and patted the bench next to him.

'How did you know this was here?'

Rob just shrugged again. 'I might have brought one or two girls down here in my time.' He patted the bench again, this time a little more firmly so the slaps echoed around the canopy above their heads like gunshots. From high up on one of the branches a bird took off in fright, its peaceful home violated. It screeched, but whether in fear, anger, or warning Beth couldn't tell. 'Come on, you might as well take a seat while we wait for those two to finish up. I won't bite, promise.' Rob smiled a wide smile, his teeth shone white against the darkening night, as if he might change his mind about that promise, as he raised his fingers to his head in a salute. 'Dib, dib, dib, Scout's honour.'

Beth glanced around at the unending moorland, the only sign of life was the urine yellow glimmer of the dome light which lit up the steamed windows of Adam's car. Even the old stone cottage had been hidden by the lie of the land, and not a single car had come along the road in all the time that they'd been there. Beth stepped into the sparse clearing, the bracken and gorse replaced by beer cans and used condoms. She perched on the edge of the bench, as far away as possible from Rob, she didn't want him getting any ideas.

But he had. He'd slipped an arm round her shoulders, trapping her arms in the oversize confines of his coat, complaining that he was cold. Trying to worm his fingers under the padded material – material she was unable to shrug off as he pressed it against her. Pushing his fingers against her waist they squirmed like slugs, clammy against the thin material of her top, as he pulled her round, turning her face towards his.

She didn't think, just pulled her head back, trying to escape from his lips that were searching for hers in the shadows of the trees, then she was whipping her head forward as fast as it would go. Pain speared through her head, she felt dizzy, as if her brain had ricocheted off her skull and was still vibrating in there. But it'd had the desired effect. Rob had let go of her. She'd stumbled back as she watched Rob stand; blood pouring from his nose, he looked like a monster out of a horror movie. She took another step back, her foot rolling on an empty bottle. She slipped and put her hand out to stop herself from falling on her back, not wanting to be prone, vulnerable. Rob took a step towards her, his hands out, before he grabbed his coat off her, causing her already unsteady balance to crumble and she pitched backwards onto her arse, her head striking the bench behind her. She fought against the darkness that threatened to engulf her, something sharp lay under her hand. The bottle had smashed under her as she fell, the neck of it poking out from beneath her. Her vision cleared as the pain lanced through her palm; tightening her fingers round the bottle, she cradled it against her. Rob spat and turned away.

Beth hadn't wanted to sit in the backseat of the car with him again, not after what he'd tried to do. Sienna would just have to swap seats, either with her or with Rob. Though Beth hadn't seen him since she'd blacked out earlier, she hoped he'd gone home with his tail between his legs, but it would be just her luck if he'd gone back to the car. He might even have persuaded the others to leave her out here. No, she was sure that Adam wouldn't just abandon her. Beth wiped the matted hair away from her face, wincing at the pain in her head. Her hand came away drenched in blood – she must have hurt herself more than she realised when she fell. She made her way through the copse of trees; in the distance the dome light from Adam's car shone and Beth made her way back across the moorland, hoping that the two lovebirds would have finished up. All she wanted to do was get home and have a shower.

She must have looked worse than even she imagined, if Sienna's scream when she tapped on the window of the car – not wanting to interrupt them if they were both still busy – was anything to go by.

'What the fuck happened to you?' Sienna leant across Adam as he rolled the window down, her top was crooked, the buttons misaligned.

She sat smoking a roll up, the car filled with a pungent sweet aroma which reminded Beth of the smell of the compost bin at home, when she emptied the first cut of the season into it. 'Where's Rob? Is he okay?'

Beth ignored the question. Opening the door, she made to clamber into the backseat, Adam's protests that she'd get blood on his upholstery hurt her ears. She didn't want to answer their questions, she just wanted to go home. Her head hurt.

'Where is he Beth? What happened to you?'

'Rob.' Beth uttered the word, but whether as an answer to either question or neither, she was no longer sure.

'Yes Rob, where is he?'

Beth's eyes glazed over; she could hear the squeal of Sienna's voice, and the lower timbre of Adam. She smiled at the thought of Adam. Why wasn't the car moving? Couldn't they see that she needed a doctor, or a hospital, or just to go home. Beth tried to concentrate but she couldn't follow what the voices were saying. Adam opened his door, leaving her with only Sienna for company, Sienna with her high-pitched whines that lanced through her brain, hurting. Why wouldn't she just shut up?

'We need to get out of here.' Adam's voice, high pitched now in fear, hurt Beth's ears as he hurried back up towards the car. She was sat on the bonnet waiting for him; fed up with Sienna she'd escaped to the comparative peace of the road. 'Someone's killed him.' He grabbed Beth.

Beth melted into Adam's arms – she'd waited so long for this moment, for him to hold her. But instead of his gentle touch, he roughly pushed her limp body away, trying to hurry her into the car. Though what the hurry could be, she had no idea.

There was a sound of gagging as Adam leant into the car and vomited. The pungent stench of the car becoming even more overpowering as he saw the mess within. He stood and turned towards Beth, his arms out. She stepped towards him, towards his embrace, but he stepped away from her, keening. Every step she took towards his open arms, he took one away, as if they were two magnets repelling each other.

'Why?' Adam kept on repeating it over and over again. The question becoming nonsensical, nothing more than a letter 'Y' repeated, thrusting into her brain.

She'd waited for him, couldn't he see that. She pulled the tire iron out from behind her back, she'd always thought she wanted Adam, but she was wrong. What she wanted was peace. She raised her arm in the air, the peace shattering.

It was late by the time she got back. Beth had a momentary pang of guilt as she remembered her mum's soup, cold now, sitting forgotten by the side of her. She locked up Adam's car; it was good of him to lend it to her and she didn't want anything to happen to it while it was under her care.

Silently she slipped the key into the door, wincing as the lock clunked as she turned the handle and tip-toed into the house. She eased her shoes off and closed the door behind her.

'Who's there?' Her mum's voice echoed through the hallway.

'Just me Mum.'

'Elizabeth?'

Beth bit her lip against the retort of *who else* that buzzed round her head.

'I'll be in in a bit mum. I need to go and have a shower.'

'Surely you can come and say hello first. Don't you want to spend some time with your dear old mum?'

Beth stopped, one foot on the stairs and one in the hallway, and surveyed her visage in the mirror. She really ought to go and have a shower first.

'Elizabeth?' Her mum's wheedling voice, needled into her brain.

Beth's hand tightened round the banister as she called back. 'Coming Mum.'

|Slipping|

It was fine at first, just slightly irritating as it slid down my heel, the material bunching under my instep, nothing but a slight crease pressing against my skin. You wouldn't know from looking. I wasn't limping. I wish I'd stopped then. Crouched, gripped at the baggy elastic at the back of my trainer sock – loose from one wash too many – and yanked it back up. It would have been quick, no one would even notice me doing it, down and up before anyone saw. Now though that slim edge of cotton had inched its way down, rolled into a ball under my sole, causing me to wobble each time I lowered my right foot down onto the dirt. No chance now of a quick yank to reposition it. Now I'd have to stop and undo my laces, but with my hands cuffed behind me there was no way I'd be able to reach them, let alone undo the knot. So now I hobble along with the others – or at least I hope I'm keeping up with them – no one has shouted at me to hurry along, so I presume that I've not fallen behind, but I can't see much through the bag they shoved over my head, only the dim burn of the sun as it sets in front of us, and if I glance down, my sneakers, one with the pink edge of a sock peeking above, the other nothing but naked skin.

I'm not sure how long we've been walking; it must have been early afternoon when it happened. I'd just finished my lunch – sandwiches, water, and an orange, if you're interested – and had wandered off to find a bin, and have a sneaky fag. I screamed of course. We're told to scream "Fire!" so that people are more likely to come help; less likely to think it's kids playing games, or that they'll be in danger themselves if they come to help. But when something actually happens you don't think about all that, you just scream. Though I've had plenty of time to think about what would have happened if I'd done things differently, if I'd screamed fire, or kicked at the attacker, or ran away; rather than freezing, whilst they grabbed my arms and yanked them behind me, cuffing them, the plastic ties cutting deep into the flesh of my wrists. I pull against them now, they dig deep into the fat.

In my head I hoped that I could remain stoic, that I would look like one of those girls in the horror films. You know, the "Final Girl", cute but not too slutty. But no, I'll look like the piece of crap I always do. Red welts digging into my fat wrists, a rash on my thighs where they've rubbed together. The denim shorts – fine if I sucked my stomach in and sat in a slightly reclined position – were not meant for walking miles in. My face is red and sweaty, blotchy and scratched from the rough hessian, caked with snot. My God! I bet my mascara's run. I probably look like a fucking panda.

I stumble. A hand roughly grabs me and yanks me upright, as I feel a foot from behind graze the back of my heel. Grit embeds itself between the creases of skin, with each step my sneaker rubs the rough dirt against my Achilles tendon making it burn. Just my luck, I'll end up with a blister now too. They never show that in the films though do they? No matter that the girl was out at a party with her friends; she's still able to run for what seems like miles from the killer, or the monster, or whatever. Never gets a blister, or cramp, or out of breath. I wish I hadn't thought of that. Now I can feel every muscle in my body tighten, each one now feels as if at any moment it'll cramp up, a real charley horse that'll have me on the floor. And my lungs are burning – as well as the skin between my thighs. If I get out of this I must go to the gym. And that bloody sock has slipped even further, the seam rubbing against my little toe, scouring away the skin, if we don't get where we're going soon I'll have two blisters, one on my heel and one on my little toe. I fucking hate blisters, for something so small they hurt like a bitch. I hope we stop walking soon; no, on second thoughts, scrap that. I hope we don't.

I wish someone would say something. It's the quiet that's really getting to me. But there's been nothing. If I listen closely I can hear the sound of gravel under feet, and panting breaths, but that could be my own laboured breathing. It's really disorientating having your head stuck in a bag, really messes with your perception. My eyes now only focus on the woven mesh an inch before my eyes; if I look down at my feet, they seem miles away. I try wiggling my toes to reposition my sock, but the sensation seems as if it is happening to someone else, a long way away; my toes, raising bumps along the dusty canvas of my shoes, look like kittens squirming in a sack. The kittens get closer, larger, cats now. The mewling sound they make reverberates in my ears, a keening that gets louder as they get closer. Lynx now, or a wild cat, maybe even one of those tigers or panthers that are rumoured to stalk these paths, escaped from some rich lunatic's country home. Before the cat can pounce though, I feel a tightening against my neck, their image safely cut off, as their growls ring in my ears. The rough feel of the fur brushes against my skin for a second before it is released. Not fur. I've not been rescued from the tigers. It's just the sack over my head. I won't look down again, maybe if I shut my eyes it'll help. No! Even the dim light that filters through is better than that unrelenting blackness. I hope we get where we're going before night falls. No. No I don't.

I need a wee. The feeling has been building for a while. Every time I put my right foot on the floor, it rolls on the sock – it feels like when I went on that cruise with my parents, and I tried to walk on the deck. I'd always prided myself that I was good on boats, but something was off as we strolled around the ship. I could see the horizon bobbing and dipping ahead, but as I put my foot down, the floor wasn't where it was supposed to be, one step too close, then one step too far. I felt stupid as I staggered across to the rail to support myself, a real land-lubber, as others wandered happily around, smiling and laughing. My mum said it was to do with the ships stabilisers; that the ship wasn't moving as much as my eyes told me it was. The bloody sock in my shoe feels the same; I lower my foot, but the ground is there just a moment too soon. It causes me to tense my stomach muscles, and each time they relax it feels like I'm going to wee myself.

I was so embarrassed when they put the bag on my head and I screamed. I waited for the sound of giggling as they laughed at me, as if *they* wouldn't have screamed if they'd been in the same situation. Though I wouldn't have said that to them. I'd have just remained quiet and waited for the joke to be over. But there'd been no giggles at my expense. I'm not embarrassed now. I don't want to speak to them; I don't want them to answer.

I loosen my tense muscles; for a moment nothing changes as my insides cramp tighter, knotting themselves, then suddenly a deluge, hot acrid piss streams down my legs. Stinging at the raw skin on my thighs, before soaking into my one sock. I suppose at least there's an upside to my one sock slipping off.

This bag over my head smells bad. I wish I hadn't had onions on my sandwich at lunch now. But I suppose at least it covers the smells of piss and sweat. I'm pretty sure this isn't some kind of joke. There's no way that Susie and the others would have been able to keep quiet once they'd seen I'd wet myself. I wonder if Susie and the others are here too. I sort of hope that was Susie's foot that caught my heel earlier, not in some mean *at least you'll get your comeuppance too* way, but at least it would mean I wasn't on my own. Though knowing my luck we'd escape and Susie would tell the whole school about how I pissed myself.

My sock has finally worked its way down as far as it can go and bunched itself under my sole. They must have noticed. I'm walking like I'm drunk now; though maybe they just think its exhaustion. Maybe they'll stop and release me, thinking I'm too weak to fight back, then I could run, make a break for it.

I stumble, not on purpose though; maybe I am more tired than I thought. Could I run? Probably not. I feel something whip against my bare ankle, thoughts of snakes flit across my mind. I pull my foot away. It feels strange, disconnected, as if the movement was nothing but a hypnic jerk. It flops uselessly at the bottom of my leg. I slam it against the floor in horror. It can't stop. We can't stop walking. My sneaker slips back on, the looseness tight again as my foot fills the sagging material. I take another step; the shoe comes away again, the sock pushing against my toes bulges through the eyelets, working the laces looser. I lower my foot, the back of the shoe folds beneath my heel. I shuffle forward another step, as the laces tangle beneath my feet. I lift my foot, but the shoe stays behind, the laces trapped behind by my weight. I place my foot down and it rocks on the rucked-up material of that fucking sock. I've lost my fucking shoe, but that fucking sock is still gripping on for dear life, pissing me off. I lift my heel, and try to do a quick two step, catching at the rolls of material with the toe of my other shoe. Desperate to place my foot flat, not to feel the wrinkles of it contorting my foot anymore. I'd be able to think clearer, if only I could get this fucking thing off—

My foot catches, the sock twists beneath my toes. I fall. The sock still on my bloody foot, as the weak light that shines through the bag recedes and is replaced with the darkness of the earth as it comes to greet me. I stop.

|The Farm|

~

Her fingers bled as she scrubbed at the floor, sweat dripped down her neck, her hair curled into rat's tails where it had fallen from her chignon. Carefully she inched her way backwards across the kitchen, away from the closed door which led into the garden. Scrubbing, her brush making intricate circles on the square, even tiles.

God, that child could make a mess.

She stood; red marks bruised her knees, matching the red on her dress. Slowly she turned her head from one side to the other, scrutinising every inch of the floor. With a sigh, she placed her hands in the small of her back, arching, her head back, straightening, the vertebra of her spine popping one by one.

I'd only just cleaned it.

She glanced at the clock hanging on the wall. It was one of those stupid cartoon clocks where the eyes moved left to right, watching her; she hated it. She'd wanted something more in keeping, classy. But Toby had seen it in that tacky shop down in the shopping precinct and of course his father had given in and bought it for him. She'd been going to hang it above his bed, intending to replace the ripped poster he'd crookedly stuck up there. But when she'd got back from the hairdressers there it was, hanging over the kitchen window for anyone to see. She'd tried to make Steve see sense, but he was adamant that the stupid dog clock should stay, saying it reminded Toby of Sandy, before pointedly stating "This is where Sandy lived, and this is where it stays." She'd pleaded for it to be put up in Toby's room, but her husband was adamant. "Why should it? Sandy wasn't allowed upstairs."

The eyes of the clock continued to move left to right, as if looking for something she missed: a speck of dirt, a smear of soap suds. Turning away she made her way back across the kitchen towards the garden door, her hand resting lightly for a moment on the handle, before she knelt again on the wet floor, her hand joining the other on the brush, her arms moving back and forth in time with the clock as she resumed scrubbing.

I can't believe he would do this to me.

Tears of frustration spilled down her cheeks, cutting rivulets through her makeup.

He always was troublesome.

Carefully she shifted backwards to the next row of tiles; her eyes remained downcast as she studied her handiwork. "The farm" she muttered as she bore down on the brush. Her fingers stung from the soapy water, chemicals seeped through the cracks and hangnails; her perfectly manicured nails were now chipped and broken. "That's right, that's where he's gone, the farm."

She pressed her hands between the folds of her skirt, the pressure enough to alleviate the pain for a moment.

It wasn't always this way. There was a time as a child where I remember being happy. My problems started with my parents, or maybe it was with Sarah. But it doesn't really matter why they began, just that they did.

Initially I had a fairy tale childhood. My parents were so happy when I was born, cooing over me, doting on me, parading me so proudly in front of their friends and family. I don't remember a lot about this time, but I've seen the photos: the pretty dresses, hair in ringlets with bows and clips holding it in place; never a smudge of dirt or a tear; always smiling at the camera, dimples in my cheeks proving that once I was happy.

Then Sarah was born and I was no longer their little angel. She was the one they lavished their attention on; kisses covered her cheeks, as slaps suddenly seemed to cover mine.

I remember walking down the street with Mother. It had been raining all day, but finally the sun had broken through and she'd decided that we should go out before I drove her mad. It was cold, and although dressed warmly, she hadn't noticed I'd put on my pretty silk shoes rather than my winter boots. My feet were frozen before we had even gotten to the end of the road. Of course Sarah was fine, she was warm and swaddled in my Mother's arms, not made to wade through the icy puddles in thin, summer shoes.

We made our way down the high street and Mother took us into one of those huge department stores. I was bored already, expecting to be forced to stand waiting while she tried on outfit after outfit of boring clothes, but I was surprised when instead of heading to the escalators, she took us to the back of the shop where the toys were. My heart leaped as I took in the massive displays. It must have been nearly Christmas as everywhere was festooned with green and red, with a sprinkling of silver snow. She picked up a snowglobe and smiled as she shook it, white granules falling like sugar over the gingerbread cottage inside.

"Are we here to buy my Christmas present?"

"Don't be silly. You know that Santa Claus brings the Christmas presents."

Sarah was getting restless in my mother's arms, turning this way and that, trying to see all the lights and colours, woken by the excessive heat and noise of the store.

"Are we here to get a toy today then?" My excitement was high as I raced off towards the doll department, images of bows and dresses, dimples and ringlets streaming through my mind. There she stood the prettiest doll in the shop, all taffeta and velvet, on a shelf high out of my reach. I turned to ask my mother to get it for me, but I was alone, no-one was there.

It seemed like hours before I found them; I had walked past the dolls and the bears, past the soldiers with their guns, and the construction sets. I walked through the stuffy clothes department and the acrid stench of the cosmetics department, perfume and powder causing my nose to itch and my eyes to run; I wiped them away, not wanting anyone to think I was crying.

Finally I found them in the baby department, my mother's hands full of red woollen mittens and fluffy scarves, coats and jumpers adorned with rabbits and foxes and other woodland animals.

"Mother."

"Only a moment, nearly done now."

She hadn't even noticed I was missing.

In my anger I reached up to grab her arm; I only wanted her attention, wanted to know that she saw me, that she would miss me if I disappeared forever. I pulled. "Mother, I've seen the doll I want, come quick."

I didn't pull that hard. I was only three years old, but it didn't stop my mother blaming me as the hats and scarves, gloves and coats fell from her arms along with Sarah.

I never got to show her the doll I coveted. Sarah was fine; a small cut to her head, but her hair would cover the scar.

Christmas Day finally dawned and I snuck downstairs, stepping on the sides of the steps as I had learned to do to prevent them from creaking under my foot and waking Mother. The tree stood dark in the corner, waiting for my parents to come and turn on the colourful twinkling lights. The room was cold, the fire laid ready but not yet lit. I eyed the silver box on the mantel that held the matches; my fingers itched to light one and watch its dancing flame as I held it to the paper in the hearth. But I understood that although my parents constantly admonished me that I was the grown up now, the big sister, they would be angry at me for touching the matches, which they'd told me were only for adults.

Not wanting to incur the wrath of my parents on Christmas Day, I shivered as I knelt on the floor and peeked at the tags on the gifts that Santa had left for us all. Just as I had ascertained that the largest gift under the tree was for me and that Sarah's gift was only a small one about the size of a shoe box, I heard Sarah's cries from the nursery above and the soft pad of my mother's feet as she calmly made her way from her bedroom to quieten her. I smiled. For once Sarah had a reason to cry; my present was bigger and better than hers. I barrelled through the door as I heard the light step of my mother coming downstairs.

"He's been! He's been! Can I open my present?"

"Ssshhhh." She waved her hand in front of me, as she turned away towards the kitchen.

"Can I?"

"Can you what?" She fumbled with the baby as she set the kettle on the stove.

"Open my Christmas present." I rushed round the table towards my mother.

"You'll have to wait. Your banging around has already woken both Sarah and me. You'll have to wait until your father has woken, and no, you can't wake him. You'll just have to wait."

Sarah's fussing had become full blown cries at the angry tone of my mother, her shrieks undulating with the kettle's shrill whistle.

"I can hold her." I held my arms out, hoping that this would calm my mother's anger at me.

My mother turned, ignoring my open arms. I wasn't allowed to play with the baby; they didn't even seem to like setting it down in the same room as me.

"I can hold her while you make the tea."

"No!" Mother's rebuke was final.

They wanted me to be the big sister but they didn't even trust me to hold the baby. I slammed the door as I left the kitchen, hoping it would be loud enough to wake my father, so I could open my Christmas present.

As I stormed down the hallway I tried to ignore Sarah's screams as they continued to pierce the air.

We didn't have much of a Christmas that year. The turkey ended up sitting uncooked and we just had jam sandwiches for lunch before opening our presents.

Of course, that was my fault. Apparently the slam of the kitchen door had made Sarah jump in my mother's arms as she was pouring the water into the teapot, causing Sarah to be scalded on the arm. Nothing serious, but Father said she had to go to the hospital.

So there was no turkey or Christmas pudding, nothing for Christmas dinner except for jam sandwiches and a decidedly frosty atmosphere. Sarah, as always, was fine. There was no long term damage and she'd easily be able to cover the scar with long sleeve dresses.

Things started to look up as we made our way into the sitting room after lunch. Mother sat Sarah on her lap as she slowly started to open Sarah's small present from Santa Claus. I sat on the floor next to the huge brightly wrapped parcel, which barely fitted under the tree. Bright colours shone through as I ripped off the gaudy paper, excitement filled my heart as I wondered what I had received.

"A kitchen!"

"Do you like it?" My father peeked out from behind the tree where he'd been handing out the gifts. "It has everything – pots, pans, a sink to wash up in."

"Ohhh, do look," my mother cooed from behind, as I stared at the plastic kitchen in front of me.

"It's so beautiful, just like her."

I turned. In my mother's hands was a small, simple box, and inside it lying nestled in folds of velvet and satin was a perfect doll. My perfect doll.

I bit my cheek, willing myself not to cry. It was clear what they thought of me. *A kitchen.* Did they really think I was going to grow up to be a maid, washing pots and pans for a living?

She blinked away the tears that threatened to splash onto her scrubbed floor. Her parents had never understood her. If only they had bought *her* that doll, things would have been different. She wouldn't have had to compensate; no, not compensate, that's a horrible way to think about it. But it's not as if they couldn't have done that one small thing for her, not when they did everything for Sarah.

Tears sprung back into her eyes as a spasm of pain arched through her back. Standing, just for a moment, she stretched as she scanned the room, Her eyes flicking back and forth in time with the clock.

Have I missed anything?

Tick-tock her eyes moved as she decided.

Once more to be on the safe side.

Moving back towards the garden door again, she gave it a quick glance before averting her eyes. Trying to forget about the mess outside, she dipped her hand back in the boiling water.

All I ever wanted was a perfect family; husband, 2 point 4 children (a figure of speech obviously, it wasn't as if I was going to chop one of my babies in half, that would just be mad). That was why I had wanted the doll as a child: it was an embodiment of me, it was perfect, it was the me I was meant to grow up to be. But I didn't get it, and at that early age I realised that there were those who were jealous, who wanted nothing more than to stop me from being the best I could be.

I married early and we moved straight here to this cottage. I had wanted to start a family straight away, but Steve said we had to wait, that we weren't financially secure enough for children, that we didn't have the money. He found excuse after excuse; he blamed it on the cost of the wedding, the honeymoon, the house.

"Don't you want to enjoy this first?" Steve motioned with his hand at the garden, the movement causing the swing chair to rock and wine to spill from his glass, a red drop blossoming on my white linen trousers.

"Don't you want to enjoy us?"

His breath smelt of fruit, and harvest, and spice; and I became heady as the aromas mixed with his scent. It wasn't my fault I forgot my pill.

She paused, brush in hand. From the front of the house she was aware of the distant sound of a door slamming and the crunching of feet down the path. The familiar squeak of the front door announced his arrival.

She could picture him now: standing on the mat, carefully checking his shoes as he removed them one by one, before placing them neatly next to hers. Stepping into his slippers which she'd stood on the polished parquet floor awaiting his return.

She lowered her head and continued to scrub.

I kept my smile, even as Steve slumped on the sofa. "You knew they weren't 100% effective."

His hands covered his face massaging his temples.

"Aren't you happy for us? It's what we wanted. Sure it happened a bit quicker than we…"

"It's what you wanted."

I moved my hands from where they had been cradling my stomach. From mother to wife once more as I placed them on my hips, shifting my weight back so I was stood in my no-nonsense stance, my voice clipped. "Pardon?"

"Nothing." Steve stood and slowly made his way to the door. "I'm going to have a shower. It's…It's been a long day."

I smiled as I busied myself in the kitchen, sure that once Steve had sluiced away the stresses of work he would be as ecstatic about our pregnancy as I was. Good, wholesome, home cooked food was all he needed. I heard his slow measured tread on the stairs, as I ladled out the stew. Placing a bowl in front of him as he sat down.

"Are you okay? You look a little peaky."

"Fine, just tired." He raised his glass of the champagne I'd got specially. "Congratulations."

I raised my glass of apple juice. "Congratulations. To *both* of us."

"It's a boy." The bundle of mucus soaked blankets was forced on me as it started to scream. I held it instinctively as far away from my ears as my weak arms would allow.

"Here let me take him. You must be exhausted."

The days that followed were an endless parade of well-wishers, but no-one was interested in me, only in the baby. Gifts of ugly baby-grows festooned with cartoon characters or witty phrases arrived wrapped in pastel blue paper. Cards covered in dinosaurs or rocket ships covered my hospital room.

"I've bought a present." My husband smiled goofily as he snuck his head round the door. "Guess."

"Chocolates? Flowers? Oh I don't know, tell me." I smiled at his thoughtfulness. "I hope it's not underwear." I whispered so the nurses wouldn't hear, as I peaked coyly at him from under my lashes. "I don't think I'm in any shape to be showing my figure off in anything revealing at the moment."

"Nope, none of those. Here's a clue."

He walked through the door with a balloon, one of the helium ones they sold downstairs in the little shop by the café.

"A balloon?" I wrinkled my nose.

"No silly." He moved to the end of the bed and tied the balloon to the crib "What's the balloon of?"

I stared at it for a moment, it didn't seem to be *of* anything, just a boring round balloon, not even a pretty one at that, just black and white. I shrugged.

"Well, now I've got my own little boy, I wanted to start him off right so I got us both season tickets. Isn't that right Toby?" He tickled him under the chin.

"He's only just gone to sleep, you'll wake him."

"Oh by the way I've finished repainting the nursery, so it'll be ready for when you come home on Monday."

"Painted?"

"Yes. I read up on how all those paint fumes can be toxic, so I thought I would do it now to give it time to air."

"But it was already painted. I chose the colours and fabrics and got that man in to do it months ago." She thought about the soft pinks and delicate flowers that she had so carefully picked from the catalogues.

"I told you we should wait till we knew what we were having before painting the nursery. You'll love it."

Carefully I folded myself out of the car and made my way down the path. Steve rushed on ahead with the bassinet, and was already through the front door and up the stairs as I bent to unbuckle my shoes, wincing as I picked his off the welcome mat and put both pairs in their accustomed place in the hall.

"Are you coming to see?"

His voice echoed through the house and out the front door for the whole neighbourhood to hear. Gingerly I removed my coat and hung it up before closing the door and locking it behind us.

"Come on."

He didn't have to shout. I inched down the hall and eased myself onto one of the kitchen chairs. Placing my hand on my aching back as he bounded down the stairs.

"Are you coming or not?"

"Not." My smile weak against his beaming grin. "Sorry, it's all just taken it out of me. I have just had a baby you know. I'll come and look later, when I've got my breath back a bit. Would you make me a cup of tea?"

He placed the kettle on the hob, before the squalling started upstairs.

"Would you be a darling? I've had to deal with nothing but that, for the past week."

"Of course."

"You could have finished the tea first," I muttered as Steve dashed out the room.

"Hi honey," Steve called out. placing his shoes next to hers. "Where's Toby? We're running late." He loosened his tie with one hand as he pushed open the kitchen door with the other.

"Honey?" A rhythmic swishing noise filled his ears, his eyes dropped to the empty table; he sniffed the air as he made his way round the dinner table and towards the noise.

"Honey?"

She looked up from the floor, her eyes staring, as her hands continued to scrub circles of foam, bubbles bursting to reveal the square neat tiles beneath.

"Where's Toby? We'll be late for footy."

"He's at the farm."

Her eyes appeared unfocused as she stared behind him, her hands repeatedly dipping in and out of the bucket of soapy water. Her gaze disconcerted him, put him off guard; he found himself glancing behind, in case she was looking at somebody else, in case someone had come in through the back door, but no-one stood there and the door remained closed and locked.

Stepping away, he broke her gaze and peeked in the oven, but the light was off and it was empty. He opened the fridge and stared at the browning lettuce. "What's for dinner? Toby might not be having anything, but I'm starving. Is he on a school trip?"

There was no answer. He looked back over his shoulder and saw that his wife was again scrubbing the floor, her eyes still fixed on the garden door.

Closing the fridge, he glanced at his watch. Depending how far away Toby was they could probably pick up a portion of chips on the way to the game.

"Honey?" He snapped his fingers in front of her face until she turned to him. "Honey, where's Toby?"

"He's at the farm."

"The farm? Why? Is it a school trip?"

For a moment she stopped scrubbing, her hair covering her eyes, her tongue poking out as it always did when she was considering something important.

"No, not school. He just had to go to the farm." Her hands commenced scrubbing again but the movements were no longer small, neat circles. Instead, the brushstrokes were long and erratic, as she lifted the brush up in the air and then slammed it onto the tiled floor before pulling it back towards her.

"Why are you scrubbing the floor? Is dinner ready?"

"Dinner? No I forgot. I was..." she gestured with the scrubbing brush at the floor.

"What's that red on your dress?"

She stared absently down at the dress which billowed around her knees, her hand raised as she began to scrub at the stain with the coarse brush, her dress ripping, as more red soaked up from underneath the fabric. He grabbed her hand before she could do anymore damage.

"Honey, where's Toby? Is he okay? Are you okay?"

"I told you. He's at the farm."

"What farm?"

"He's gone to see Sandy." She pulled her hand away from his and stood, smoothing her torn dress. Her eyes alighted on the garden door for a moment, before she turned quickly back, picking up the bucket of still steaming water, and made her way towards the sink.

Sandy was beautiful. I saw him in the window of the local pet shop, a golden ball of fluff, paws up against the window. He wagged his tail, bounding up and down the length of his cage as I walked back and forth. He was unable to take his eyes off me, and I was equally as smitten.

"It smells."

"Come on!" I dragged him into the shop as Toby covered his nose and mouth with both hands.

"But the smell."

He started to pull backwards, twisting this way and that, trying to free himself; his reins twisted in my hands, causing a friction burn to turn red in my palm. I jerked at them, lifting him from his feet, just for a moment; not enough to hurt him you understand, just enough to show him who was in charge here.

I leant down. "The smell is fine, it's only the puppies and kittens." He wouldn't look at me, his hands which had moments ago covered his nose and mouth now covered his whole face. He was about to have one of his tantrums, I could see the signs. "Look at me." I grabbed his arm, pinching it between my fingers. I twisted, just once. He lowered his hands. "Now, that's better. Don't you want a pet?" His eyes were watering, but he nodded silently.

"Why a dog now?" Steve scrubbed at the burnt beans at the bottom of the pan. "Surely you've got enough on your plate with Toby. You're always saying it takes all of your time just to look after him. So why now?"

She lowered her mug and stared at his back. "Toby chose him. I couldn't say no."

"Since when was Toby in charge?" He sat down, drying his hands with a dishcloth. "It's not even as if Toby's old enough to look after it himself."

"I'll look after him, it'll be fine. It'll do me good anyway; give me an excuse to get out of the house."

Steve grimaced at the back garden, spade in hand. The lawn was covered in dead patches and piles of dog faeces. He'd been looking forward to getting out and getting the garden ready for summer, going out first thing, full of the joys of spring. But his joy quickly faded once he saw the state of the lawn.

"Why is it covered in poo?"

"The weather's been awful. I couldn't take Toby out in the torrential rain we've had all week, and the dog's got to go somewhere. Better out there than in here."

"But why didn't you clean it up?" He pulled the roll of bin bags out from under the sink. "It's ruined the lawn."

"The garden's not my job, it's yours. I have to do all the housework as it is. Anyway, the dog's not mine, it's Toby's. He should clean up after it."

~

"Sandy? You mean our dog Sandy?"

She didn't reply, just nodded as she poured the water down the sink. The steam billowed on the window, warping her features, causing her reflection to cry tears of condensation.

"But Sandy's dead."

"No, he's at the farm with Toby."

"Honey, he's dead. We buried him in the back yard, behind the trees, while Toby was at his grandparents last winter. Remember? We didn't want Toby upset, so we didn't tell him."

~

"Bad boy!"

Sandy cowered in the corner, shivering. Vomit caked his muzzle as his hind legs shook, diarrhoea coated his flanks. I took a step closer, as he took another step back. Another wave of diarrhoea squirted onto the kitchen floor.

"I didn't sign up to this." Grabbing the dog by his collar I pulled him out into the garden. Rain instantly soaked through my slippers and dressing gown as I stood shivering in the cold. "You're Toby's dog; he should have made sure you were house trained." I yanked him towards the stake in the ground, attaching his lead to it. Shouting to be heard over the rain and his whining. "You'll just have to wait here until I've cleaned it all up. Bad dog."

It took ages to clean up the mess. Each time I thought I'd finished there'd be more, I'd catch sight of a smear of brown, or take a breath and the stench would hit once again. At least I'd set down the law about the dog only being allowed in the kitchen; imagine the mess if it had gotten into the rest of the house. Finally, I realised that the smell was probably me and not the floor. Carefully I stripped off my slippers and nightclothes, throwing them into the bin bag with the rest of the rubbish and headed to the back door. The rush of wind and rain against my naked skin brought me back to myself. I couldn't go to the bin naked, but at least I could get rid of the rubbish into the back garden to be disposed of later when Steve got home. Gingerly I picked up the bowl of dog food and sniffed it, careful not to touch the meat inside, before tipping the contents into the bag and tying it shut.

Opening the back door the unmoving shape of Sandy was little more than a spectre through the rain as I put the trash out, before heading upstairs to run a hot bath.

"Honey, snap out of it." His skin crawled. Why on earth would Toby have gone looking for Sandy? Of course they'd told him that Sandy had gone to live on the farm, but it was just a white lie, a convenient story. Toby had never asked to visit Sandy before. "Honey, you've got to snap out of it. How do you know he's gone looking for Sandy? When did you find out? Why are you cleaning the floor and not out looking for him?"

He grabbed her by the shoulders, forcing her to face him. "If Toby's gone to find Sandy, we have to go look for him. Have you any idea which farm he's gone to?"

"The one Sandy's at."

Her eyes flicked away from him. He followed her gaze to the garden door. He stared at the wet floor and the red stain on her dress.

Slowly he made his way across the kitchen and turned the key. His hand came away tacky, he rubbed his thumb and forefinger together, some sort of residue coating them, rust maybe. He pressed down on the handle, the door swung partway open before hitting a pile of rags, more signs of his wife's spring cleaning.

"Yes! I told you he's gone to the farm. Why don't you listen to me? No-one ever listens to me. Toby's gone to live on the farm with Sandy."

|Non-Standard Construction|

~

Room to let. The card lay crooked behind the dusty pane of the corner shop window, resting against an aging silver Christmas tree crowned with a lopsided angel, whose smile did little to dissuade you of her feelings about where the top of the tree had been wedged. Strangely enough – though it was strange in itself to have a Christmas tree on display in the middle of summer – the tree was surrounded not by presents, but by an array of stuffed rabbits, straw chickens, painted eggs, and a children's plastic bucket and spade.

James nearly walked past, leaving the yellowed parchment to curl up and die on the fly festooned window ledge, but this was London and accommodation was hard to come by, at least in his price bracket. He couldn't afford to ignore even the slightest chance of finding somewhere to rent.

James opened the door to the shop and stepped inside, ducking to avoid hitting his head on the bell that hung loosely above the door, as if someone had tried to rip it from its frame. Whoever had unsuccessfully tried to tear it from its moorings had plucked its tongue out instead and the bell swung gently in the morning breeze, voiceless. Another step depressed the stained camelhair mat and a buzzer echoed from the back of the store announcing his presence.

James made his way towards the counter where an elderly woman stood, watching. He smiled, trying to show he was friendly, that he was harmless. He still wasn't used to the general miasma of mistrust that seemed to permeate every corner of this city. The people who seemed to watch your every movement, each nuance catalogued and assessed as they measured you against a rule. To check you as not bad, or evil, that you weren't going to harm them, rather than whether you were good or kind. *There are no saints here*, their faces seemed to say; *no reason to do good just for the sake of it*. If you committed a good deed, it would be because you had an ulterior motive, that you wanted something in return. *There are no saints here.*

James felt the smile wither on his face under the woman's scrutiny. She opened her mouth to speak and a jumble of words came out in a deep, echoing timbre. The woman wasn't a woman; the dress, some kind of robe; the make up, dirt encrusted in wrinkles which were too deep to be cleaned by a cursory wipe of a cloth; the breasts, nothing more than the ageing chest of an overweight man who looked ready for his grave. James was glad he hadn't spoken first, that he hadn't named this strange creature made sexless by age as a woman. That he hadn't given the shopkeeper a reason to dislike him more than he already did.

James indicated behind him at the window. The shopkeeper continued to gabble, his peculiar voice given gravitas by James' incomprehension of the words. The man remained where he was, unwilling to leave whatever small amount of security or prestige the counter gave him over his customer.

James reached into the window, past the sun bleached boxes of laundry detergent he was pretty sure weren't even made anymore and the strange display of faded festive cheer. Hooking the card between his fingers, he retrieved it to show the old man.

The shopkeeper held out his hand. James made to pass him the card, but the old man closed his withered fingers as if they were a mouse trap springing sharply back, and whipped his hand away, cradling it protectively against his chest. The card fluttered down from James' slackened grasp and landed prostrate on the scratched and graffitied plastic countertop. James stared at the back of the card; white as a baby tooth it gleamed unsullied against the faded names and announcements scored and gouged into the peeling Formica. James turned his face back to the shopkeeper, whose hand was back again outstretched, his eyebrows raised in silent question. James lowered his hand to the card in front of him. The gnarled face in front of him shifted, the brows drew down, the tattooed grime disappearing into the deepening furrow of his brow, as the shopkeeper slowly shifted his head from side to side before bringing his thumb and forefinger together and rubbing them in the international sign for money. James opened his wallet and peeked into the empty change compartment; the only items his wallet currently held were his oyster card and a five pound note. He pondered for a moment as he stared at the fiver. It was expensive enough living in London and he was in two minds whether to hand over the money for what might end up being a hopeless endeavour. The flat might be too expensive, or in one of the dodgier parts of the city, or even worse it may already have been let. He fingered the slippery material of the note before pinching it between his fingers and offering it to the shopkeeper, hoping that he wouldn't offend the man. He'd heard that the new money was made from animals, and he had no idea whether the note was kosher or not, but then again he had no idea if the man in front of him was Jewish, or Muslim, or Christian – he could be Pastafarian for all he knew. It didn't seem to matter, however, as the five pound note disappeared into the folds of his robes.

The shopkeeper turned away, as if aware that this stranger had nothing of any further worth, and continued to stock the shelves. James picked up the card from the counter and turned it over hoping that it wouldn't be another waste of time, and that this wouldn't be his local shop when he finally managed to find somewhere to live.

Room to let. The elegant cursive stated only that, and on the back a number.

James had always wanted to live in the city. He hadn't exactly burnt his bridges when he'd left home, but they were definitely smouldering; his family and few friends fed up of hearing about how everything was shit, and how much better off he'd be once he was out of there. He hadn't been in London long enough yet to be willing to turn tail and flee back to the single bedroom at his parent's house and his (presumably now ex) fiancée. He'd given her an ultimatum, and she hadn't made the right choice, so there was no way he was running back up there. He'd wanted the excitement of the big city and that was what he got. He'd settle in soon enough, he just wasn't used to London yet.

On his first day he'd woken early, excited; with the old adage *the early bird gets the worm* in mind, he'd been up and out, searching for a coffee and waiting for the estate agents to open. But the shutters were down as he walked passed row after row of closed businesses, the owners either long gone or asleep, he couldn't tell. The first signs of life he'd witnessed had been the doors being unlocked to a pub on the corner. Its windows boarded, the door, a dark aperture, a mouth that swallowed him whole as he made his way in. Picking up yesterday's paper from a table he'd ordered a coffee, which arrived lukewarm. Sitting himself at a table underneath one of the grimy lights he'd squinted at the newspaper, circling the rooms to let. He tried the first number but the call wouldn't go through; turning the phone so the light shone on the screen, he saw one bar, not enough to make a call. How in the capital city he couldn't get a signal he couldn't fathom. He'd pushed his mug away, the tepid liquid spilling over the stained porcelain, and picked the paper up to head outside and find some daylight and a signal. As he headed out the door the barman cleared his throat and put his hand out. James had wondered for a moment what the man wanted – he'd already paid an extortionate price for the drink, so it wasn't that he was welching on the tab.

"Paper please."

James stared at the barman "But it's yesterday's."

"Papers are for all the customers. Not fair on the others is it? You haven't paid for it, it isn't yours."

James glanced round at the empty bar before reaching into his pocket and bringing out some coins. He dropped a pound into the barman's hand, and it disappeared without an offer of change.

He'd headed outside, the day now warm, but the streets were still empty as the daylight struggled to penetrate through the high buildings and reach the ground, leaving the roads in a perpetual gloom. He phoned every one of the numbers in the paper, and each time he was met with the same answer – he was too late the flat had gone. It didn't matter how small, how expensive, whether it was above a knocking shop or next door to a prison, the answer was always the same; you should have been quicker, the property had been let.

James turned the card over in his hand and took his phone out of his pocket, praying he'd got enough minutes on it to make the call. The last thing he needed with his money running low was a huge phone bill.

The flat wasn't let. The cracked voice on the end of the line had told him the property was still available and given him an address, telling him to be there that night at nine on the dot. So here he was, making his way through this scarred and defaced landscape, visions of violence flashing through his head. He couldn't see how the dregs of society managed to afford houses in London anyway – for all intents and purposes London should be a haven for the middle and upper classes; the disengaged, the destitute, the deranged, priced out of the city. But still he walked along the streets he couldn't afford to live on. Saw them thronged with chavs and druggies leaning over their garden walls, flicking cigarette ends into the gutters that were full of excrement from either the dogs or the children that ran amok, unfettered and unattended in the alleys and pathways that threaded their way round the backs and sides of the shuttered and blinded buildings.

Finally he arrived at the address he'd been given. The property sat squatly beneath the surrounding high-rises. The streetlights cast shadows on the render causing the ugly house to look leprous, but it had four walls and a roof, and at the moment James wasn't in a position to be picky about where he lived.

Footsteps clicked down the pavement towards him. Turning, James saw the woman heading towards him. He expected her to turn and cross to the other pavement as most people seemed to down here. Willing to take those few extra steps to avoid confrontation. But instead the lady raised her arm in salute, a clipboard held in her hand. As she made her way closer she called out his name, and as he nodded in response she ticked something on her list before heading down the path towards the house.

"How much is it?" James knew it wasn't smart asking the price straight up. He was sure that the woman would sense his desperation and boost the price to more than he could afford, but he didn't want to get his hopes up again.

"£250 per calendar month." She ticked something else off her list. "Plus deposit of course." She reached a manicured hand past his head and flicked a switch, illuminating the mottled walls with a sickly yellow glow.

"Seems cheap." The words were out of his mouth before he could stop them.

"Non-standard construction." She unlocked the door to the right of the hallway and James squeezed past her and stood by the bed. In truth, wherever he stood in the room he would be by the bed – the room was tiny, with a double bed against the far wall, a single wardrobe to one side, and a single bedside table on the other. The space smelt musty, age had yellowed the paper and damp had patterned it with black curlicues of mould. James opened the wardrobe; the back of the door sported a rust-spotted full-length mirror. James reckoned he'd have to stand outside to be able to use it to any effect, and even then it would still cut his legs off. The wall to his right featured a huge window, overlooking what he supposed was the garden. A row of overflowing bins stood like sentries looking in. "Are the rest of the rooms let?" he asked but the room was empty, a voice echoed from the bottom of the hall.

"The kitchen is down here and the bathroom is upstairs."

He made his way out of the room, switching the light off and carefully shutting the door. Pushing it to make sure the latch had caught, he headed down the dreary hallway towards the kitchen which smelt like socks and week-old takeaway.

"Everything you need is here – cooker, microwave, fridge freezer. You have a shelf each in the fridge," she opened the door, the light shone on her face as she screwed her nose up at the sights that greeted her, shutting it quickly before heading towards a list laminated on the back of the door, effectively cutting him off from seeing whatever was lurking inside the fridge. "These rules are set by the landlord for the benefit of the tenants, as long as you stick to them…" she pointed at the laminated list, her finger touching it for a second before she quickly withdrew it and surreptitiously wiped her hand on her trousers "…you'll have no problems with the others."

"You're not the landlord…landlady then?" James watched as the woman ticked a final box on the sheet.

"Oh no, I'm just his agent, he doesn't like to be bothered with all this." She circled her pen in the air. Turning the sheet over, she thrust it towards him, indicating a line on the back of the paper. "Sign here."

"Don't you want my references?"

"I'm a good judge of character. You can move in tomorrow if you pay cash up front for the first month, or we can wait until the bank has cleared your first cheque."

"Cash is fine." He hoped he had enough in his overdraft to cover the first month's rent – he'd be living on noodles and beans for the rest of the week until he got paid, but it was worth it not to have to fork out the money each day on the hotel. He took the proffered pen and signed his name.

The next morning he was waiting bright and early at the property. With his belongings stuffed into a rucksack and a variety of carrier bags, he looked like a homeless man. Which he supposed at this exact moment in time he was.

He bit at the skin round his thumb, stripping off tiny strips, a drop of blood welling from where he'd been worrying at the tender flesh.

Once he'd left the property last night, James had stopped at the bank, withdrawing the maximum he could; on the way here this morning he'd stopped at the same cashpoint and done the same. He hadn't checked his balance to see if the money was available, he'd just bitten his cuticles down to the quick and prayed that the machine would spit out his money and give him his card back. It'd been too late, then too early, to actually go into the bank and speak to a human being if his money had been refused, and he didn't think it would have done his cause any good anyway, standing there like a hobo with all his belongings at his feet. Banks didn't seem to give people like him loans, but thankfully he hadn't had to try; he'd folded the wedge of notes into his wallet and stuffed it deep into his pocket, keeping one hand on it to make sure he didn't lose it.

The house was no prettier in the bright light of day. The ageing guttering sagged across the upper windows, which were blinded like cataracts by sheets pinned up inside. He glanced at the naked eye of the window where his room was situated. The first thing he'd do this weekend was put some proper curtains up. He wasn't a student anymore, and as he had no idea how long he'd be calling this place home, he might as well make it feel like one. The sun shone on the pocked grey walls, but rather than making the house more inviting, it instead showed the full degradation of the building. Decaying render lay in lumps on the brown grass exposing the inner rot and decomposition of the wall beneath. He headed over and poked at a particularly large patch next to the front door.

"Concrete cancer."

He turned, his finger coated with the white powder residue to see the agent stood behind him.

"Nothing to worry about, it's common in non-standard construction."

"Non-standard construction?" James mused out loud.

"Nothing to worry about, lots of houses round here are non-standard, because of the bombing in the war."

The words meant nothing to James, he had no idea what she meant, but he nodded along, hoping it didn't mean the ceiling was going to come crashing down on his head while he slept. Because this was it, he had to move in, he couldn't afford to live out of hotels for much longer, and he wasn't going to head home so soon after showing his friends and family the finger. Anyway if it was no good he could always save up some money now he wasn't wasting it on hotels and take-outs, and find somewhere better. This was just his first foot on the ladder...

"...and our number's on the back in case of emergencies."

The agent dangled a key attached to a green plastic fob in front of his face. James realised he had been nodding along for ages and hadn't taken in a single word the woman had been saying. He wondered if he should ask her to repeat herself, but instead found himself reaching for the key and uttering "Thanks" as he stepped forward to open his front door.

Exhausted, he'd been on autopilot when he left work, and had gotten halfway back to the hotel before remembering that he didn't live there anymore, turning round to trudge back the way he'd come. He always seemed to feel worn out after work these days. Although he did nothing but sit on his arse and watch screens, he found the nights monitoring the CCTV exhausting. But it was only a stopgap, money to pay the bills, while he figured out what he really wanted to do, and it wasn't as if he'd actually got the money or the friends down here to have any kind of social life anyway.

The sun was up when he finally got back to the house; the rooms quiet as he slipped his shoes off and padded up the stairs in his socks, hoping to grab a shower before the rest of the house stirred and there was a queue for the bathroom. He'd lucked out so far, hadn't seen anyone from the other flats, occasionally hearing a muffled step on the stair or a distant voice, but the other tenants were as elusive as ghosts. He ran the shower and waited for the ancient pipes to clank into action and the trickle of water to heat up. Stepping into the shower, he felt the base of the cubicle gritty under his feet. The shower had a thick layer of dust, white patches spattering the lower edges of the glass cubicle where the water had hit it and flicked it up. He used his foot to scoot the now-white water towards the plug hole, waiting for the sludge at the bottom of the shower to clear before ducking under the showerhead and washing.

James towelled himself off and grabbed his toothbrush. Turning the tap on, he watched as the water spattered against the dusty porcelain, white rivulets running across the grimy sink. James ran his finger through the thick layer of dust in the unused sink. He was sure that there was only the one bathroom. The agent hadn't mentioned more than one. Maybe, he thought to himself as he spat the minty foam out and rinsed the sink clean, the other rooms had sinks in them which the other residents used, or maybe they all had dentures or really bad breath.

James woke while it was still daylight outside. He yawned and wiped the gritty sleep from his eyes. The room was bathed in the auburn warmth of the sun as it peeked over the surrounding rooftops. He allowed the warming rays to engulf him as he lay on his bed – he didn't have work tonight, but he'd got no real idea what he was going to do. He probably shouldn't have slept so late, but he couldn't be bothered to realign his body clock for just a couple of days a week. Anyway since moving down here it wasn't as if he knew anyone, so it didn't really matter whether he was awake during the day or at night. He switched on his phone and flicked through the announcements from the few old friends who still spoke to him: *Going to the local* ☺ *...again* ☹ *bet*

you're having more fun down in the big smoke. Can't wait for the invite. James glanced around at the cramped bedroom – there was no way he was going to invite his mates to stay here, they all thought he was living the high life, not stuck in some dead end job and living like a bloody student again. He flicked through to see if there was anything worth going to locally: nothing. He checked the movie listings, and then the prices, and remembered the state of his bank balance. He didn't even have enough money for a pint at the pub, let alone a night out. He switched on his laptop, but without any WiFi it was useless. Making a mental note to sort that out first, once his next pay check cleared, he closed the laptop again.

Through the wall he could hear the muttered conversation of his housemates. It wouldn't hurt to go and introduce himself. The worst that could happen would be they'd have nothing in common, in which case he could pretend he was just grabbing a glass of water and head back to his room. But they could be cool, maybe they'd even know of a party or something, anything to get him out of the house – well, as long as it was free.

He shoved his feet into his trainers and glimpsed at the shorts and t-shirt he'd slept in; they were wrinkled but he decided not to bother changing, worried he'd miss his chance to speak to the people in the kitchen. He scurried out of the room and made his way to the kitchen for a cup of coffee and to introduce himself. But the room was empty, the kettle cold as he picked it up to fill. Placing it back down in the black circle which was set into the dust on the worktop, he wiped at the residue with his finger before glancing up at the ceiling to find the source, but the swirling patterns which stared back at him appeared undamaged.

The house wasn't all that bad, certainly not as bad as the house he'd shared as a student – the sink was always empty, and apart from a strange smell, the fridge appeared to be clear of rotting food. The only problem was the dust.

He'd cleaned the kitchen down the night before, before unpacking his shopping. It had looked as if someone had been baking, and spilt flour everywhere. White dust covered every inch of the work surfaces, gummed to a paste under the constantly dripping tap in the sink. He'd wiped the surfaces down before unpacking his meagre culinary delights: some cheapo noodles, coffee, and baked beans, alongside a single bowl, plate, mug, and a mismatch of cutlery.

But wiping the sides down obviously wasn't enough, because the kitchen was once more covered in dust again.

James rooted about in his cupboard for a bowl and one of the packets of noodles he'd stashed there. Running his finger around the inside of the bowl, it came away white, and when he glanced in the cupboard the contents all had a light dusting of powder on them, as if they were doughnuts sprinkled with sugar.

James ate standing at the sink – he could have sat down, but the table and chairs were all covered with the same white dust, and he didn't really have the money to take his clothes to the laundrette unless he really had to. He hoped that the voices he'd heard earlier would return; standing in the ever-growing darkness, he waited for a sign of occupancy from the house. Finally, after his third cup of coffee, he admitted defeat and washed his plate and mug up, placed them back in the cupboard and made his way back to his room, his shoes leaving footprints in the dust on the tiled kitchen floor.

James woke the next day and wiped at his sleep-encrusted eyes. He was starving – glancing at his phone, he saw that it was just after lunch. "Fuck" he thought to himself as his stomach growled at him.

He'd wasted his day off yesterday. Bored, and with no money and nothing else to do, he'd picked up his book to read, but as the sun set he'd found himself falling asleep, although he'd only been awake a couple of hours. Now here he was awake in the middle of the day – he'd slept for a solid twelve hours and there was no way he was going to manage to fall back asleep, and now his body clock was fucked. He'd be crap at work tomorrow night.

He lay in bed and rubbed at his eyes again, they still felt gritty. He spat on his fingers and wiped at his eyes in an attempt to unglue them, but they felt sore and irritated. Sitting up he ran a hand through his hair, white dust flew like dandruff around his head causing him to cough. He glanced up at the ceiling but there was still no sign of damage to the swirling artex. *Must be old dust I've disrupted, moving my stuff in* James thought to himself as he brushed the powder from his skin. He stood and stretched, glancing at the mess in his room. He edged his way past the bed and over the scattered carrier bags that littered his floor, and made his way into the hall, opening the cupboard under the stairs. "Got nothing better to do" he muttered, pulling out an antiquated vacuum and a plastic bucket filled with some equally ancient cleaning supplies.

It was getting dark by the time James had finished cleaning. He felt better than he had done for ages; the house felt fresher, he felt like he'd gone and done a workout at the gym, and finally he'd managed to eradicate all the dust.

He stowed the vacuum back away under the stairs. Secretly he'd hoped that someone would have heard the noise and come out, but either no-one was in, or – more likely from the state of the place – no-one wanted to get roped into doing the cleaning. James' stomach growled again; he hadn't eaten since the noodles last night and what he really wanted was a pizza, but all he had left to last him till tomorrow was a tin of beans and yet another packet of noodles. James decided to head upstairs, grab a shower and get himself clean, before settling down in the kitchen to his meagre feast.

Turning the shower to its highest setting, James noticed that the metal showerhead was again shrouded in a fine layer of dust. Wetting his hand he wiped it, cursing himself for missing a spot, before he stepped under the tepid water.

James felt drained as he made his way home following work – a twelve-hour shift with nothing to eat was bad enough, but with his body clock out of sync, and it being night, there was nothing to distract him from the ominous creaks and groans of the building. It had been tortuous. At least he'd had coffee, but he'd drunk so much of it, his stomach felt like acid. He'd only gone to the loo before leaving work, but still he needed a piss and he was only halfway home. Trying to hold it in without grabbing himself and looking like a perv, he gritted his teeth, striding down the street, counting the steps in his mind as he hurried home. Once back he threw open the door and ran up the stairs to the bathroom. Not bothering to remove his shoes and tiptoe up quietly, uncaring if he woke the other residents. He'd seen neither hide nor hair of his housemates since he moved in, and was beginning to think that he was the only person in the house. To be honest, with working nightshifts he hardly saw anyone – he couldn't be entirely sure that he wasn't the only person in London. For a bustling metropolis it could really be dead at times.

He flushed the loo and made his way to the sink to wash his hands. The soap felt greasy as he lathered it between his palms, and glancing down he saw that his hands were peppered with grit. The sink once again had a layer of dust across its porcelain surface. He rinsed his hands and wiped them on his trousers before turning off the tap and opening the bathroom door with the sleeve of his jacket, white streaks contaminating the cotton. He'd been looking forward to stocking his cupboards with food from the shops. It was payday and for once he had enough money to eat well for the whole month, as long as he didn't live on takeaway. But the idea of preparing food in the filthy kitchen turned his stomach. Gingerly he pulled the front door to and headed towards the greasy spoon cafe he'd passed on his way home.

The greasy spoon wasn't too bad, in fact it wasn't greasy at all, the food was fresh, and the place spotless. James pushed aside his orange juice and toast and powered up his laptop, typing in the café's WiFi code. The waitress didn't seem to mind him taking advantage of their hospitality as the place was empty following the breakfast crowd, and it would be a couple of hours before the office workers started to make their way in for their lunchtime sandwiches and salads. He clicked on the icon on his laptop and waited for the internet to boot up; he'd been intending to update his CV, but instead found himself typing *non-standard construction* into the Google search bar, hoping he might find out a way to stop the incessant dust from falling. He scrolled through the results with one hand while he picked a piece of toast up with his other, a white residue lining his nails like a French manicure. He placed the toast back on his plate and picked up the fork, trying to squeeze one of the tines down close enough to the nail bed to get out the entrenched grime. A drop of blood fell onto the laptop's keyboard, he winced and went to place his finger in his mouth before thinking better of it and wrapping it in a serviette instead.

He clicked on the first link and read through the article. *A deficit of housing after the war lead to an increase in non-standard housing materials, concrete being the most common.* As he scanned through the article, words such as cancer and asbestos jumped out at him; he grabbed the keys out of his pocket and dialled the number on the plastic fob, tapping his fingers on the table as it rang. He'd heard all the horror stories about asbestos, the scarring of people's lungs and them dying, gasping for breath. He thought about the dust lying thickly on every surface, the dusting on his pillows in the mornings, the grit in his eyes. How much had he inhaled already? Were the walls of his lungs already beginning to thicken and scar?

A voice trilled down the phone line, he fought back the need to cough as he spoke to the agent.

"Of course there's no asbestos."

"But the dust… It's everywhere."

"If there was asbestos, it would have been picked up in the survey. All of our properties have to be properly checked, and if they contain asbestos, we have to put a sign up."

"What about the dust though, it's getting into everything?"

"I'm sorry about that, but cleaning isn't included in the monthly rent. You'll just have to come up with a cleaning rota or something with the other tenants."

James hung up and swallowed his final mouthful of orange juice; his throat tickled as he fought back the urge to cough. Unwrapping the serviette from around his finger, he squeezed the nail between his thumb and forefinger. The skin beneath throbbed at the pressure and a tiny indent in the white infiltrated the pinkness beneath his nail. It felt as if someone had stuck a pin into the tender flesh there.

On his way home James popped into the supermarket, but instead of buying food to stock his shelves, he bought polish and bleach. Having filled his basket with every type of cleaner he could find on the shelves, he made his way over to the cashier, baulking at the extortionate cost as he passed the cash over; he'd be eating nothing but beans and noodles again for the next month. He just prayed that the new cleaning stuff would finally shift the dust in the house.

Once home he rooted through the under stairs cupboard and pulled out the plastic bucket, tipping the old cleaning supplies in the bin. He filled the bucket with warm water and a liberal slosh of each of the cleaning fluids he'd picked up at the shop. He hoped that the new stuff would work better – the old stuff had probably been there years, looking at the state of the house. It had probably gone off. He hoisted the bucket and headed upstairs to start cleaning.

James was scrubbing the skirting boards in his bedroom when the phone rang, he wiped his soapy hands on his shirt before picking it up and swiping to answer. The screen felt grainy under his touch, a scratch marring the surface where he'd run his finger across.

"Where are you?"

"In my bedroom." James wondered at the question. "Why?"

"Cause you should be here. At work. I was due to knock off half an hour ago."

James pulled the phone from his ear and stared at the time – he was late, it had taken him longer to clean then he'd expected. He apologised profusely to his boss and, grabbing his bag, he rushed out of the house.

"Last warning."

James' boss looked him up and down. James was all too aware that he was wearing the same clothes as he had been when he'd left work that morning, the only change being the splashes of bleach which spattered his trousers, the black material flecked with coral and amber and saffron, like a sunrise on his crotch. Dust sprinkled his shoulders like dandruff: he was a mess, but at least he was here. He couldn't afford to lose this job – what with paying for the hotel and now the deposit and the rent, he had no savings to see him through until he could find another. He locked the door behind his boss, and ran his hand across the rough stubble of his chin before settling down for another long night of work.

He woke suddenly, the vertebrae in his neck popping as he straightened, a cold cup of coffee congealing in front of him. He moved it to see the screens, but they were empty. A hammering echoed further back in the building. James picked up his torch; he didn't need it for its light – the building's fluorescents were on sensors which lit up the corridor ahead of him as he made his way towards the source of the noise – but in lieu of a gun or a nightstick, the heavy metal tube would at least make a decent weapon.

The hammering emitted from a metal fire door at the end of the corridor. James pressed the handle down and the door swung swiftly away wrenching his arm. James stumbled forwards into the ample bosom of the cleaning lady.

"What, were you asleep?" The cleaner barged past him, heavily bundled in her coats despite the mild morning air. "You've made me late." She reached the staff room and turned, her finger pointing at him as if marking him "It won't be me that gets it in the neck." She slammed the door behind her as James made his way back to the reception. Unlocking the front doors he waited for the others to arrive.

James hurried home; his body was weary and ached from all the cleaning, and from falling asleep at his desk. His rucksack bounced against the tight muscles in his arms, sore from all the scrubbing the day before. He'd managed to sneak away without the cleaner tattling on him to his boss. At least if he was going to get a drumming from his boss it wouldn't be until he was rested, clean and in fresh clothes.

Finally home, James trudged up the stairs. Too tired to shower, he intended to brush his teeth, grab some water and sleep. He squeezed toothpaste onto his brush and turned on the tap. The water ran into the sink, disturbing the thin layer of dust. James ran his finger across the sink, coating it in the white residue. He rinsed his finger and glanced around the bathroom. From a distance it all looked fine, but he was sure that there was a fine coating again across the top of the toilet cistern, and along the edge of the tiles. He rinsed his brush and swallowed some water. It tasted brackish; he'd have to pick up some bottled water to brush his teeth. He just hoped that boiling the water would get rid of any impurities, there was no way he could afford bottled water for his coffee too. James took in the room, his features drawing into a moue of disgust. He lifted his hand to his mouth, his teeth biting into the calloused skin round his nail and pulling a thin strip away. Pain bloomed in his finger, blood welled against the side of his nail, flecks of white slowly engulfed by the red liquid. The white line on his nail bed had lengthened, reaching almost to his cuticle, and the pad beneath was fleshy and hot. He hoped it wasn't infected. He rinsed his finger in the sink, not wanting to put anymore of the white stuff near his mouth.

James made his way downstairs, the banister sandy beneath his palm. He glanced at the closed doors along the hallway – maybe the dust was coming from them. Maybe he should slip a letter under their doors asking them to clean their rooms. Ha! He sounded just like his mum. Maybe he should knock on their doors, wake them up, demand that they keep the house clean. He'd heard that in the city you were never more than ten foot from a rat, maybe he should round some up and plant them in their bedrooms, that'd give them some motivation to keep the house clean. But not today. Now he wanted nothing more than to climb into bed and sleep.

James woke to the muffled sound of his alarm. He rolled over to switch it off and his chest heaved, causing him to cough, a wad of phlegm flying out of his mouth. He didn't feel good, his throat was sore and irritated; he swallowed to try and lubricate it, but every time he swallowed he coughed, which caused his throat to burn even more. He rubbed his eyes and flakes of sleep fluttered to his chest, but still he couldn't open them. Gently he probed at the swollen, hot orbs; wetting his finger with saliva he rubbed at them, carefully prising them apart. He shuffled into the kitchen and turned on the tap; pain flaring through his fingers as he gripped the faucet, he cupped his burning hands under the water and drank. It tasted worse today than it did yesterday. He gritted his teeth and splashed the cold water on his face, hoping that it would do something to alleviate the burning.

James made his way back to his room and picked up the phone; he dialled work and waited for it to be answered.

"Hello, you're through to Solutions. How can I help?"

James opened his mouth to speak but no words would come out. He tried again but his throat burned too much, was too damaged. He tried a third time but his voice was drowned by a barrage of coughs. He hung up and texted his boss instead, before switching his phone off and pulling the covers back over his head.

It was dark when James next woke; a coughing fit wracked his body as he sat up and threw the covers back, dust motes dancing in the moonlight that shone through his still uncovered window. When he rubbed his eyes, the skin on the back of his hands felt rough, flaky. Glancing down, he saw eyelashes clogged with thick clots of sleep caught against the scaly plaques of skin which covered his hands and crept up his arms. His throat burned, he needed to get some medicine, he reached for his phone to check the time. Missed calls flashed across the screen accusingly. He'd been asleep for thirty six hours, he'd missed two days of work, and thirteen calls from his boss. James deleted the voicemails without listening to them, and winced at the last text message which just said *You're Fired*. James switched his phone off – the black screen veiling the condemning words – before he climbed back into bed and pulled the duvet over his head.

"James?" There was no answer from behind the bedroom door. "It's Sally, the lettings agent." Sally hoped that James wasn't in. She hated confrontation, and would rather get the locks changed and his stuff boxed up and out into the garden before he came back. She didn't really want to be here at all, but the landlord was adamant. The payment hadn't been on time, and there were no excuses. There was always someone more than happy to find somewhere affordable to live in London. She turned the key, and the stench hit her. It reminded her somewhat of the nursing home her Nan had been in – bleach, with a heavy undertone of rotting flesh.

She stepped towards the window, meaning to open it and air the room, her hand covering her mouth as her eyes wept in the stinging fumes. A body was hunched over in the corner by the wardrobe. Her heart sank as she saw the grimy clothes, the head hung low, the stench of rot – a miasma which emanated from the body. She'd have to call the police and the family. It was the part of the job she most hated, having to clean up after the tenants. She headed towards the body, praying that there wouldn't be too much puke or blood. Its head turned at her approach and red rimmed eyes met hers. A hand raised in greeting. Skin cracked and raw, the hand dipped back into the bucket at its side, tendrils of red mixing into the milky liquid as it squeezed the cloth, before returning to scrub once again at the sparkling clean floor.

|Origami|

She smiled as she watched him. His fingers usually so slow suddenly nimble as they floated like butterflies across the colourful paper.

It was times like this that made it all worthwhile; she hated the stares, but even worse were the pitying glances she caught out of the corner of her eye, or the well-meaning comments whispered across to her from friends and strangers alike.

I don't know how you cope.

Like her son, she never engaged. She simply smiled and quietly guided him away.

A zoo of animals sat around him, elephants, rabbits, cranes. He'd drifted again, disappeared back into his own world. His fingers now just folding the paper repeatedly in half. She'd read somewhere that it was impossible to fold a sheet of paper in half more than nine times. She tried to count them as his hands swiftly turned the paper, one, two, three… each one followed by a neat pinch and fold – his hands hypnotic, her eyes so tired – she blinked and missed one, two, three? She tousled his head which remained bowed in concentration; there would be no response today, no smile, no frown, not even a break in his routine as he folded and smoothed, folded and smoothed.

Her hand remained there a moment, the feel of his hair now coarser beneath her fingers, no longer the soft down of childhood. She could see the shadows starting to appear on his chin and cheeks. She wondered where the years had gone, where he had gone, as she made her way past him into the kitchen.

The kettle boiled, water poured into mugs; tea for her, chocolate for him. She placed a couple of biscuits on the plate, hoping that the sweetness might draw him out for once. Steam rose from the mugs, twisting as a breeze came from the lounge. A frown puckered her brow and for a moment she wondered if he still looked like her when he frowned, his brow puckered in dismay as his fingers betrayed him, turning a delicate crane into a predatory pterodactyl.

Leaving the drinks to cool on the counter she stepped through the door into the lounge, the room empty, the window open; the only sign of his previous occupancy a stairway of paper leading out to the moon.

|In and Out the Dusty Bluebells|

~

I've always loved spring. It's a new start after the cold, dark winter months. There has always been something special about it for me: whilst most children were excited for Santa, and sparklers, and snowfall, I was just counting the days until it was warm enough for me to wear my shorts to school. But my mum always seemed to deem it too cold, and I would have to beg her, pointing out the girls who were already in their gingham dresses, rather than their stiff starched pinafores. Those gingham dresses, as blue as the bluebells that thrust through the ground in the woods, were always to me the first sign that spring had truly arrived.

In and out the dusty bluebells…

As I got older, though, that sign of spring abruptly stopped. One year I'd begged my mother to allow me to wear my shorts to school – I'd been pleading for weeks, that winter had been an especially bleak one for me. Moving up into secondary school, I'd thought it would be exciting, but my only friend had ended up going to the posh school at the other end of town, leaving me alone in the local comprehensive. Finally she relented. Unable to find shorts that fitted – she said it was because they didn't make them in my size; I countered, that if she'd bought them when I originally asked, they wouldn't have sold out – she took up my school trousers from the previous year. As I watched her cutting away at the frayed cuffs, I was glad that she'd be unable to tell me to wear them on art days anymore, when she complained about the paint and the glue that inevitably became smeared and entrenched into the grey material. Now at least the other boys wouldn't laugh at me for wearing ankle flappers.

But when I arrived at school on the Monday morning – early for once, beaming from ear to ear, my knees frozen, the fat marbling like corned beef – it wasn't to the sight of gingham dresses with matching scrunchies holding up dishevelled ponytails. It wasn't to the sight of knees scabbed and bleeding, imbedded with gravel, from races run and scuffles fought, those signs of power in the playground hidden by grey polyester. The only knees on show were the pristine knees of the girls who'd rolled their skirts up at the waistband, flaunting themselves as they flaunted the rules of the school and their parents.

Their mockery was worse than usual that day, their taunts and laughter even more cutting than when I'd worn my old trousers for art class. I persevered through the day, blocking my ears from the names, but unable to block the kicks that rained down on my bare legs, bruises blossoming like petals on my pale flesh. I snuck out the back gate from school and ran across the muddy sports field, my muscles aching as blood pumped through them, aggravating the bruises, turning them as blue as the bluebells that grew in the ditch around the edge of the field.

In and out the dusty bluebells...

The bluebells are now my only sign that spring has truly arrived. Of course the girls still put on their gingham dresses, and the boys still wear their shorts. But it is seen as bad taste for an adult to watch the school too closely for these signs of spring. It is frowned upon by society to be seen to be too involved with the enjoyment of children, unless they are your own. It's sad: what could possibly be more of an apt sign of spring than seeing the children skipping in and out of each other's arms, hands clasped together, as their bodies entwine and their voices sing angelically the songs of their youth. Those signs of spring – of hope, of new starts, of new life – perfectly embodied in the simple games of the playground. Though of course even before, when I still watched the children playing – before the women at the school gates stared to ask which child was mine. Before they asked if they were in the same class, the same school year as their own child. Before the teachers started to watch, waiting to see if when I was the only person left at the gate, I came to find where my son or daughter might be. Before the headmaster approached me and asked if he could speak to me, privately, in his office. Before the entreaties to leave; before the threats of the police, of the fists of angry fathers, of the community – I knew that those angelic smiles could turn to sneers. That those gay laughs could become sniggers held behind grubby hands, that those same grubby, sticky hands could turn quickly from holding yours in play, to swift, painful, pinches.

Unlike the parents at the gates, beaming at their little angels, I hadn't forgotten the games that the children liked to play at school when their parents were no longer around and the teachers were safely ensconced in the staff room.

So now in the winter I walk the woods, waiting for those first signs of spring. The first year I came here there was very little sign of any life. The ground was thick with rotting leaves and dog shit and little else. The wildflowers of my youth, those unsullied snowdrops, those garish daffodils, and of course my favourites, the bluebells, were conspicuous by their absence.

The lady who owned the tea shop at the visitors centre told me that the council had dug them all up when they were putting in the new accessible path, and that they'd never grown well anyway, the ground was too acidic or alkaline, or they didn't get enough light, or something like that. I personally thought that was shit – though I didn't say that to the tea shop owner – that it was just an excuse because either the local council had run out of money, or couldn't be bothered to replant them. I started to tell her about how I remembered the spread of colour across the glades, that as a child I had come up here to marvel at the beauty of spring, those delicate bluebells which dappled the ground with their vibrant colour, their blue heads held aloft on gently bobbing necks of slender green stalks… But I must have been boring her, as the lady made an excuse about having to get a cake out of the oven before it burned and rushed away whilst I was still mid-sentence. So I sipped my tea. Calling goodbye as I stood to leave, but my only answer was a clattering of pans in the kitchen; so I pulled the door silently closed behind me, shoved my hands deep into my pockets and surveyed the damp woodland through the gentle mizzle of rain which had commenced whilst I was in the tea shop.

I didn't want to walk through the dank woods with nothing to mark the changes of the seasons except the slow rot of leaves, and the hardening of mud into dusty soil. So I made a promise right then, that each year I would plant a patch of bluebells. Though the lady at the tea shop was right about one thing, the flowers didn't really like the soil. Their heads wilted, and their colour mottled as quickly as I planted them. Each year I tried a different area of the woodland, or a different genus of bluebell, *Campanula rotundifolia, Hyacinthoides non-scripta, Mertensia virginica*. But none of them flourished, until I found the special ingredient. It was the soil you see. It needed to be fertile for new life to spring forth. It had been neglected and left barren for too many years. It needed nourishment if the plucky little flowers were going to manage to thrust their way through the hard ice-packed ground each spring.

In and out the dusty bluebells…

I did think about getting a dog. No one thinks twice about a man with a dog walking in the woods, no matter the weather. They just think that you're caring, that you've put yourself out to ensure that the dog gets what it needs. No one looks at you strangely, as you trudge through the snow, or turn your collar up against the rain that gathers and falls in pregnant, freezing droplets from the canopies above. There would have been no need to come in the bitter early hours of the morning, or late at night when the only people out are the dog walkers, the joggers or the teenagers high on drink and drugs, flirting with each other on the rusty old playground. But then again people may have still looked at me strangely as I walked through the woods, shovel in my hand. I thought about hiding it out here, but I only need it when I'm planting and I was worried that someone might find it, steal it. Then when I needed it, it wouldn't be to hand, and I'd have to get another, and I didn't want to have to go all the way back to town just to get a new shovel when it was imperative that I get my compost and flowers planted before the frost damages them.

In the end I decided against a dog, they're too unpredictable, they are supposed to be loyal, but with my luck it would probably have turned on me at the most inopportune time. Sure it might have helped me with meeting women, I suppose they might have found the dog cute, even if they didn't find me cute. But in the end I didn't need a dog to meet women. As I said, in the mornings there are plenty of joggers about – although I do avoid those that look too fit, it's not kiss chase, and I don't want to be running after women all day. Anyway, it's not as if I'm flitting from one woman to the next.

You shall be my partner.

I dig the hole, ready to plant. It's a deep one this year, six feet by two feet by two feet, but it is important to remember when planting bluebells to ensure that their roots are deep enough to protect them from the frost.

|Piggies|

I think it probably stems from when I was a child.

No, I wasn't a particularly anxious child, well not until I was a teenager. Up until then I'd been pretty happy-go-lucky. It wasn't anything huge back then either, I just swallowed my tooth. I'd been eating toffees in the playground, got them hidden up my sleeve so the teachers wouldn't see and confiscate them, and the other children wouldn't see and ask me to share. Well, one of my teeth was loose, it had been wobbling back and forth for days – you know, one of those teeth that you push horizontally forward with your tongue until your parents tell you to stop it or they'll take you to the dentist to have it pulled out. Well, I was eating my last toffee in the playground when it happened. The toffee wrapped itself round the tooth as I chewed and with a dull pop and the taste of copper flooding my mouth the tooth finally came out. I spat it into my hand; the tooth was thoroughly embedded in the toffee. I suppose I could have sucked it off, but the bell was about to go and I knew I'd get in trouble if I was called on to answer any questions and I had a mouthful of sweets; I didn't want to throw it away as my mouth already tasted as if I'd been sucking on pennies rather than candy, from the bloody gap where my tooth once stood, so I put it back in my mouth and swallowed the lump down in one, the butteryness of it coating my throat as my tooth slid into my stomach.

No, it wasn't swallowing the tooth that caused me any anxiety, it wasn't like the woman from the nursery rhyme who swallowed a fly, where she panicked and ate more and more, bigger and grosser creatures until she popped. It wasn't an accident you see, it was deliberate. I chose to eat my tooth, to swallow it down. No, why would I think it was gross? It came from my mouth, and I put it back in my mouth; it wasn't like I plucked it out of someone else's head or found it on the floor. That's when I can pinpoint it starting. The anxiety happened later. It was a by-product… no, not even that, it was just something that happened, you know? Exams, parental divorce, bullying. The holy trinity of stressors for teenagers. But the stress *is* what caused me to start biting my nails.

My parents did everything they could to stop me. They tried withholding pocket money, bribing me with treats – you know, small crap, like money for a movie, or a trip to McDonalds. They made me paint my nails with that foul tasting stuff, my dad even painted them bright red, telling me that if I was going to make my nails stand out and look like shit, at least he could make them look pretty. He only did it once. I'm not sure if it was because he felt guilty at the black eye I got from the other boys at school, or if it was because I just moved on to chewing the dead skin round my nails instead. Yeah, I suppose the nail polish did work to an extent. I had no issue with eating my nails – same as with the tooth, they were a part of me – but I had no idea what kind of toxic chemicals were in the nail polish. I didn't want to end up poisoning myself. Anyway, I suppose it did stop me biting my nails for a while, though they probably looked worse to my dad then than they did when I bit them. They ended up super long. I checked them against my friend's. Paige was one of the nerds, not a cheerleader – they weren't allowed long nails in case they gouged someone's eye out when they were reaching out to catch the flyers. No, she was one of the art students, straight As in all her classes, so the teachers let it slide if she flaunted the dress code. She had gorgeous, long nails – fake of course – which she decorated painstakingly with Easter bunnies, snowflakes or as bloody talons, dependant on the time of year. She was going to paint mine, until I ended up ripping one out from the nail bed. No. I told you, I didn't eat it, didn't know what chemicals were in the cheap shit nail polish my dad had slapped on it. No I threw it in the bin. It came off as I had no idea how to do anything with long nails. Holding a pen, throwing a ball, having a shit – long nails just got in the way. Scratching and poking and bending. I hadn't been intending to grow beautiful long fingernails, it wasn't a middle finger to my father and his patriarchal idea of what was or wasn't gender appropriate. I just forgot. I hadn't cut my nails myself ever; my mum had done it when I was younger, snipping them neatly on a Sunday evening after I had a bath, and since I'd been biting them, there had been no need, so I just didn't think to do it.

My mum bought me one of those finger socks, the ones that look like a condom that you slip over your finger to stop it getting infected. Well it worked, at least for a while. It was about a month later when she asked me to take it off so she could have a look. I'd told her I'd been checking it when I had my shower, and I had, I'd replaced the dressing each day, though I'd poured that disinfectant crap she got me from the chemists down the sink... not all in one go, just little by little so she'd think I was using it. That stuff stung like I'd stuck my hand in a wasp's nest, and it tasted like shit. Anyway, after that she took me to the doctor They were obviously stumped – no pun intended – there was no sign of infection they told her, but the wound definitely looked larger than they would have expected purely from someone losing a nail. They insisted on bandaging it up properly and made me promise not to remove the dressings, but to come in every three days to get it checked and replaced.

I watched the nurses closely as they unwrapped my hand, watched what they used to clean the wound with – saline if you're interested, no bloody foul-tasting disinfectant, just plain old salt water that fizzled almost pleasantly as it flowed over my raw nerves – what they used to dress it, and asked them what signs of infection they were observing for. My parents were pleased at my interest – they'd been expecting a sullen complaining teenager, instead of the polite boy who sat still and watched so closely as my hand was wrapped and unwrapped like a burrito several times a week, my mum proudly telling the nurse that I wanted to be a doctor when I grew up; it wasn't that, it was never that, though I never said anything to dissuade their belief, that the reason my room was piled high with books on anatomy and dissection, that the reason why my internet search history – at least the one they could see – had articles on tourniquets, cauterisation, and amputation. I did nothing to dissuade them that my hours alone in my room were anything more than me being a conscientious student, and by the time my grade card came in it was already too late. But it wasn't that.

The reason, the only reason, was because infected flesh tastes rank.

～

I think they thought I would grow out of it. They watched me carefully for a while, but they had no idea; the closest they got was probably thinking I was suicidal, that it was self-harm, a shout out for help. But it wasn't. I was a generally happy kid: anxious, but happy. I had friends. Sure, I was bullied, and there was a crap six months after my parents separated where they both just tried too hard, each trying to show me that they still loved me, that they had only fallen out of love with each other, not me, how could they fall out of love with me, their son? I thought about asking them why they thought they couldn't fall out of love with me. They'd chosen to be together, to get married, to start a family, and they'd still fallen out of love, but me I'd just happened, they had no idea what I was going to be like, a jock or a nerd, a priest or a rapist. As the song says *We could have been anything that we wanted to be*. It wasn't the thought that they could fall out of love with me that ramped up my anxiety then, to be fair I couldn't really have given a shit, I was a teenager and if you think I hadn't fallen out of love with parents at that age, then you've forgotten what it was like to be a teenager. It was more that their love was smothering me. It was as if they thought swaddling me in cotton wool and spending every spare minute with me would make up for the time that I was at the other parent's house.

It was hell, it would be hell to any teenager. You want to spend your time with your friends, you need your privacy for… well you know what for. I don't have to spell it out for you. But it was even worse for me, my nails were already bitten to the quick, the skin round them ragged and torn, the cuticles clotted and scarred, the nails never growing quick enough to assuage my hunger. Much to my father's disgust I'd grown my hair long, and though he refused to make me cut it, probably worried that I'd refuse to visit him at the weekends if he did, he muttered about it under his breath. Every Friday when he picked me up from Mom's, he would suggest a trip to the barbers the next morning.

It's amazing how many hairs you can pluck from your head without people noticing. The first ones were just wrapped round the elastic I used to tie it back at school, they pulled as I tugged it from my hair as I was about to shower after soccer, the sensation oddly soothing, like when Paige sat behind me and plaited my hair, her expert hands weaving and tugging, tickling and cool against my skin. I unwound one of the hairs, amazed at the length of it, as I rolled it between my fingers, forming a fur ball no bigger than a sprinkle. I popped it in my mouth. After that I pulled each hair out carefully, the sensation of release as the root came away was almost as pleasurable as the sensation of the hair within my mouth. Some I wadded up together and ate like marshmallows, others dangled individually like a liquorice lace. I managed to keep it to that until I was at college and out from beneath my parents' watchful eyes. Probably the only person who actually cared enough to notice was Paige. She'd comment on how thin my hair was as she plaited it, wrapping the fine strands around each other, her fingers tangling in the knots and wisps of hair that grew back sporadically from their damaged roots. She spoke of self care and conditioners, of not letting my parents get me down, that I should relax more. Her fingertips massaged my scalp as her voice soothed me. The thought of her not being able to twine her fingers through my hair, of that one physical contact that she allowed between us to be broken, was the only thing that stopped me from going completely bald at school.

By the time I left for college my parents were resigned to the fact that their son was never going to be a doctor – my grades nowhere near good enough for pre-med – though I think they still harboured some hopes, especially when I got my EMT and started working the weekends. My mom was happy as she thought it would mean I was less likely to be out drinking; my dad was happy as he thought I was doing it to earn some extra beer money. But neither was really the case, it was just a means to an end. You couldn't go stealing the morphine or anything like that, but pain has never bothered me, and no one noticed if you were several dressing packs light at the end of a shift.

It was the training though that was a godsend. I knew just where to fix a tourniquet, and although the videos I watched weren't part of my training, it's amazing what you can find on YouTube these days, and no one questions why you have a scalpel if you look like a medic.

The scars healed well, the incisions small and neat. I paced myself back then, allowing each one to heal until it looked no worse than an acne scar, before making my next incision. Each time taking no more than a sliver from thigh, or chest, or hip. Each time careful to avoid the arteries that threaded their way through my body, the blood gently weeping from the minuscule cuts, each morsel as revered as caviar or foie gras, a treat, the rarity of it making it all the more special.

My anxiety was better since leaving home, whether it was being away from the overbearing love of my parents, or the smart comments from the dullards at school, or whether it was because I was now able to indulge my hobbies in peace. I didn't know and didn't care, but I did make a concerted effort to stop biting my nails, no one wanted an EMT with ragged, bloody nails, and I certainly didn't want to risk picking something up from one of my clients. My body was my temple. In the same way that people want to know their steak has been treated well, or their eggs are free range, I wanted to be sure that the meat that I was eating was healthy.

It's ironic that at this point I became vegan, at least, as far as everyone else knew. I'd heard that herbivores had a sweeter meat and I wanted to see if it was true. As an aside, it's also a great way to save money in college. It wasn't until I passed out at work that I realised my diet was unhealthy. When they ribbed me for being vegan, I'd told people – a smirk upon my lips – that I ate an alternative protein, but the small incisions I was making, although sweet, weren't enough to keep me going. The body needs protein to repair, and the balance was out in my food intake. Also, sometimes you just need to break your diet, you want to eat dirty, you want a pork chop or a chicken wing; you need to be able to pick your food up with your hands, to get sauce down your front and feel the meat fall from a bone.

I washed my feet carefully, a bowl sterilised thoroughly at work, sealed and smuggled home, warm water laced liberally with salt. A sterile apron lay on the ground next to it, a dressing pack open, paper towel, gloves, scalpel, all in an orderly row, everything I could possibly need to hand, there was no getting up and popping in to work for bandages, or popping into the kitchen to sterilise a needle in a pan of water. Once I was started that was it until the job was done. As they say: butts in seats, head down and concentrate; procrastination is for losers. I lowered my right foot onto the paper towel before slathering my hands in sanitiser. I wasn't sure if this would be like losing a finger off my right hand rather than my left, was the fact that I was going to excise the littlest piggy off my right foot going to be worse than if it had been my left. There's been no useful information on the internet, and when I'd practiced, pressing down on my toe with a sharpie to see how steady my hand would be, it was my right little toe that was the easiest to reach – other than my left big toe, but the internet was sure on one thing: I'd adapt better to the loss of my littlest piggy than I would my biggest.

The pain? Oh the pain was nothing, no worse than if you catch yourself in your zip after going to the toilet. No, it was the blood that got to me. I thought I was going to die. The plastic was slippy with it beneath my feet; as it spread across the sheet and inched towards my dorm carpet, my first thought was *fuck, my deposit!* but my second was quickly fear at the amount of blood I was losing. I now know that there wasn't *actually* that much, it just seemed a lot spread out like that. There probably wasn't much more than what seeped out from the slivers I sliced from my body, but puddling on the plastic it looked far worse than when it was soaked up by the wadding I'd hold beneath the quick cuts I made in my fat and muscle. I hate to admit it, but I threw up. I think it was that or pass out. I was feeling rather woozy; at the time I thought the dizziness was due to blood loss, but I know now it's because I'm just a wuss when it comes to the sight of blood. I don't even like that fake, bright red corn syrup you get in the horror movies, but the dark viscous liquid which bubbled up from my foot was far worse.

Yeah, the wound's a bit shit on my right foot, I ended up just pressing wadding against it, and wrapping it in bandages. I couldn't hold the needle, it just kept slipping out from between my bloody fingers each time I pressed it against the skin to stitch myself up. Anyway, it healed, I managed to sneak some antibiotics from work without anyone noticing, and I took them just in case of infection, but whether it was down to my prep or good luck or the antibiotics, no infection set in, even with my crappy makeshift dressing. The wound on my left foot is much cleaner. I wadded that one so the blood didn't end up everywhere; a sanitary towel beneath the foot, worked a treat.

The only problem is I was two down, and to be fair there isn't really much meat on a toe. Far less than a chicken wing, more like those fancy frogs' legs you get in posh French restaurants.

Well, after that I had to make a decision. There was an imbalance – I needed protein to heal but my body just wasn't getting enough from the little piggies. The wound size in relation to the meal was out, you have to be careful, there has to be parity, calories in versus calories out, as any good nutritionist would tell you. I know the next logical step would be a finger, but there's still not much meat on one. An arm or a leg would be better, wound circumference to meat quota would be much better, but if I cut off an arm this early I'd really struggle later on, and as for a leg, well, I'm a young man, I didn't want to end up in a wheelchair for the rest of my life. But taking into account the amount of meat versus wound size – without sounding too boastful – I decided there was only one option really. I didn't have a girlfriend, and the idea of a wife and kids all seemed so far away; the urgency wasn't there in the same way as my hunger was, so I cut. I forgot quite how many nerve endings are packed round there. I know, I know, pleasure equals pain, *Yada yada yada*. It just didn't twig that those two things were caused by the same thing. Of course I knew at an academic level, but by then any rational thought had gone out of my brain. You know how they say you get 'Hangry'? That your mental function slows down if you don't eat? Well that's what was happening to me. Then I woke up here. Yeah, my roommate found me. No, I don't care what he says, the bloody shit stirrer, I expect he's told everyone on campus by now. Yes, I realise that I can't go back. Yes, my parents are picking my stuff up today. That prick who I shared a room with insisted that I go. Said he didn't trust me, couldn't sleep in a room with a *sexual deviant* like me.

I just want to set the record straight: it wasn't a kink, that never came into it, I was just hungry. Oh, that reminds me, what time's dinner? I'm starving.

|To See Sweet Cate Cry|

The words made no sense, their voices raised in a sweet harmony as they skipped round the circle, hand-in-hand they danced as one, serpentine in their revolution, an ouroboros that surrounded her. Eyes averted, she stared at the cracked tarmac beneath her feet. The breeze catching up grit, sandblasting her bare legs and billowing her gingham dress as if she was a balloon about to float away. Cate grasped the material in her scratched and scraped fingers, blood staining the check as she held it down demurely; one hand at the front, one twisted round the back to spare her any more embarrassment than she had already been subjected to. Suddenly the voices stopped as they turned as one to face her; their arms raised in supplication, as they moved in to envelop her.

It was the bell that stayed their hands, balled into fists, and their feet shod in patent leather. As one, the children straightened and filed off, giggling and skipping hand in hand to line up at the door. A Pavlovian response to the sound of the bell, order instilled on the disorder of a moment before. Miss Beasley tutted in disapproval at the sight of Cate as she hurried to join the back of the line, her pigtails askew and dust streaking her dress. Cate put out her hand to grasp that of her partner in the line, but no one took it, no fingers entwined with hers as she stood there. Arm held out at 45 degrees, she filed past Miss Beasley, her tuts pursuing Cate into the cold corridor beyond. Miss Beasley didn't follow; she just stepped out into the playground and made her way across to the pile of rags that lay in a heap where Cate had left them when the bell rang.

Each sat with their own. Tables for two stood in regimented rows; Cate took her newly assigned seat alone at the front of the class. Behind her the susurration of whispered voices echoed at the edges of her hearing, words muffled but their intent fully understandable to Cate as she looked at the empty seat beside her. She glanced up at the clock, hands twisted on the desk in front of her as she focused on its ticking; counting down the seconds until Miss Beasley returned, the minutes until she could stand once again and leave those shrill voices behind, the hours until she had to once more take her place in the circle.

From out in the playground came the sound of singing *Ee I de antio, the farmer wants a wife* the familiar words accompanied by the familiar squeak of the caretaker's wheelbarrow as Miss Beasley pushed it across to the ever-growing compost heap that lay behind the sports hall. There was a rumour that last year someone had jumped from the roof of the hall onto the compost heap beneath; even now with a year's extra waste tipped on it, it only reached a third of the way up the wall. The rumour went that last year a Bone jumped, trying to avoid their fate, but that they did nothing more than break both their legs, and were ceremoniously dragged off the heap by Miss Beasley, and wheeled round by her in the wheelbarrow until it was time for the circle once more. But then there were other rumours: that it was sweet but simple Simon that jumped, not realising that those that goaded him had no intention to follow. That he broke his neck, and instead of his parents being told, he was left there to rot with the rest of the rubbish. Or that it was Jack, his name carved as Head Boy on the wooden board that adorned the wall behind the teachers' table in the dining hall. His story, less gruesome than the others, speaks less of a jump than of a flight, of feet settling square upon the top of the heap, before he nimbly made his way down, his story a legend. At least until next year, when another name would be gouged into the wood beneath his, and Cate presumed the stories would begin again.

Cate wondered if they changed year to year. Whether theirs was the first to whisper them behind hands in the changing rooms and playground, in those hallowed and harrowed spaces where the teachers left them alone. Or whether it was hereditary, built into the psyche in the same way the circle was. No one ever met those in the years above or below. It was how the pairing worked. It was how it had worked for as long as anyone could remember; her parents had been paired, as had her grandparents. Cate remembered her first day at school, her eyes shining as she scanned the yard. She'd hoped for love at first sight, the fairytales that her parents had told her each night before she fell asleep. But none of the other children caught her eye, they all seemed too boisterous, running after each other, grabbing at hair and bottoms and breasts like animals. Cate had hidden behind her parents as one boy reached out to grab her; her parents stepped aside, but it was too late and the boy was already away, grabbing a girl and smushing his face against hers, as her screams were cut off by his lips. "George!" Teachers ran across the playground to break them up. Tears ran down the girl's face as her parents fished out hankies from their pockets and dabbed at her eyes, cooing at her to stop crying, to make herself presentable for her first day, that it was only for a year, and look, she'd made her mascara run all down her face.

Cate risked a glance behind her. The voices fell quiet, heads bowed, eyes down at desks as if the other students were reading books that only they could see. The desk where George had sat was already gone. The other desks shifted to hide its absence. They were only a quarter of the way through the year, but already half the desks had been removed from the class, stacked in a cupboard off the assembly hall, locked away so as not to remind the remaining pupils of what was gone. The teachers muttered between themselves that they'd never had a year like this, a year so bad, so wrong. But still they didn't intervene, each day they stood watching as the children formed the circle, hands entwined, their voices raised in sweet song as they skipped round in play.

Cate didn't tell her parents about her day, about the names that the others called her. "Flea bag. Dog. Bitch." She didn't tell them about the boy who'd been sweet on her, and was now lying behind the sports hall, just because she didn't like him that way. She didn't tell them how now no one liked her. That she'd spent her day alone. She didn't want them to worry. She wasn't sure if they would worry even if they knew, or if they'd even grieve when she was finally gone. But she decided to spare them that, at least for one more day – they were her parents, and she loved them, even if she wasn't sure if they loved her. So she pushed her barely-touched plate away at dinner, and begged an early night, blaming her pale countenance and lack of appetite on her period, before creeping away to bed, where she lay awake until the sun bleached the stars from the sky.

Cate was exhausted when her alarm went off. She was tempted to tell her parents she was sick – a night of worry and no sleep would certainly help her play the part – but instead of dragging the covers back over her head, she got up and sat in front of her dressing table. Opening the pots of shadow and rouge she readied herself for the day, covering up her exhaustion with layers of foundation. She rimmed and shadowed her eyelids to detract from the red veins that mapped their way across her sunken eyes, slashing at her mouth with the ravishing red lipstick her mother had bought her for a gift on her first day, the one she'd never had the nerve to wear before. Slipping on a fresh dress, Cate stared at her reflection in the mirror. She didn't recognise herself, painted and powdered, a doll stared back at her from the mirror, its face expressionless beneath the layers of makeup that drew her countenance into one of acceptance and acceptability. Revulsion gripped at Cate, but she stayed her hands as they reached for the tissues to wipe her face clean and naked, to show herself once more. Today was a good day to be someone else, to be anyone other than her.

The giggles started as soon as she stepped through the gates. Sly glances and fingers pointed at her as she held her head high, eyes wide as she fought back the tears that threatened to flood her at any moment, her gaze distant and aloof as she avoided meeting anybody's eye. Crossing the playground, she stood in front of the large wooden door and awaited the bell that would signal the start of the day.

Miss Beasley stared at her as she rang the bell, its pealing a harbinger of what was to come, a herald of beginnings and ends. Cate watched through lashes heavy with mascara, but Miss Beasley didn't look away, her eyes tracking Cate's approach. Cate thought she saw a flash of pity in those eyes, but then it was gone, hidden behind Miss Beasley's cold stare. Cate filed past, fighting the urge to look back over her shoulder in the hope of catching her teacher unawares. She wasn't sure what would be worse if she did look back: to see the pity on her teacher's face, for the acknowledgement of what waited for her when the bell in her hand rang once more, or the blank, uncaring stare that she was used to. Standing behind her lonely seat, she waited for the remaining children to file in two by two.

Cate stared at the composition book in front of her, the lines blue like veins, unsullied on the virgin page, as she listened to Miss Beasley speak, the words distant, the ticking of the clock above the door echoing like thunder through her head, counting down the seconds until Miss Beasley would ring the bell once more and they'd all make their way outside for recess. Thankfully – either because of sympathy or simply because she no longer mattered anymore – Miss Beasley didn't call on Cate to answer any questions that morning. She just left her to stare blankly at her empty book and contemplate her fate.

Cate jumped to her feet when the bell rang and hurried out. In a way she was glad it was over, she'd lived this moment hundreds of times since yesterday. With her back straight to avoid creasing her dress, and a smile on her painted face, she made her way over to the edge of the playground and stood, hands extended, by the bloody patch of dirt that marked the centre of the circle.

James strutted into the centre of the circle. His smile wide, wolfish and confident in his standing, as he waited for the circle to close.

Hands reached out, Cate's fingers betrayed her. Aware that there was no happily ever after within her ending, her body still yearned for the touch of another, and her fingers closed around the hands of those that stood next to her. Feet lifted, Cate found herself carried round to where she began once more. Voices chanted. The circle broke as Peter stepped up to Jill and claimed her as his wife, the hierarchy of the community singing in joy as, one by one, they joined together to sing the words, until there was one. Cate waited as their voices rose in unity, their song sang so sweetly, as they called her for their Bone.

|Places to Run, Places to Hide|

~

I sit waiting in the early morning light; even now the sun's already hot against my neck, the caress of the warm breeze how I imagine a lover's touch would feel, kind and intimate. The toe of my sneaker scuffs at the dust as I trace unknown shapes in the surface, shapes that I obliterate and reform as I wait to walk along the road.

A shadow emerges from the early morning haze. I can see no features, but I know who it is, I will always know who it is. Usually there are more, but today – for reasons unknown and uncared for – there are just the two of us. We are friends but it is enough.

I stand and stretch as I wait for him to arrive, and without a word we turn as one and continue back up the road, empty this early in the morning, but soon it will be full of those who have a routine – school, work, shopping, the monotony of daily chores; for today however we are free, and when those others appear we will be far away from them all, away from the drudgery of daily life, away from those unwanted glimpses of what our future holds for us. For now our future is undefined, our desires unnamed, and we are free from other's ambitions; our yearnings a compass which may lead us anywhere.

We pass our usual places, our dens and hidey holes, as if realising that today is special, different from those that have passed before. Today the world is ours, new and reborn; because of this our time must be spent wisely, searching, finding, yearning for new places, new sensations, new experiences. Today is not a day for repetition but a day for wonder.

We don't speak as I pass him a headphone, walking in unison, separate but together, joined by the music which we share. As if in payment he passes me the cigarette he has been smoking. I draw the sweet, musky smoke deep into my lungs, my lips touching where his have moments before, savouring the taste before passing it back.

As one we pass the waking world, apart, separated from them. My heart aches in my chest as if I am holding my breath, tiptoeing past so that the world does not know where I am going. It is a sweet soulful feeling, a secret feeling, building as I make my way past the edge of town, turning from the main street onto the path which will lead me away. As I step on the loose gravel the feeling breaks in my chest, exhilaration suddenly fills me like a well. I break away, ignoring his cry as the headphones pop from our ears. I can't stop myself, I run, free, unencumbered, for a moment not caring what anyone thinks or feels, for at that moment there is no one else, there is only me. My feet beat out a tattoo on the gravel, and all I can hear and feel is the beat of my sneakers on the dusty road. Slowly the heat of the day envelops me, and I stop, my hands on my knees, my heart beating in my ears, sweat dripping off my face, as I wait.

He walks past me, not slowing his pace, his displeasure at my show of independence evident in the stiffness of his walk. *It is fine to be different as long as you are the same as me*, his countenance seems to say. *I am the leader, not you.*

I shrug to myself and trot to catch up. I am sure at some point I will regret this perceived slight to the hierarchy of our group, but I will deal with it at a later date. It has happened now and there is nothing to be gained from directing attention towards it. Switching off my stereo I wrap the headphones around it and put it away in my pocket; we walk in a silence which neither of us is able to break.

The heat of the day presses on me as I continue on our pilgrimage, placing my hands on my knees I push myself up the hill, fighting through the overgrowth on the path. My senses are assaulted by the scents that surround me, greens and yellows, dusty pollens which tickle at my nose, the stringent scent of nettles crushed beneath my feet. My breath catches in my throat as I make my way through the pungent miasma; overwhelmed by sensation I struggle to place my feet one in front of the other. Each step takes me away, higher above the town; slowly I make my way up to the summit.

Suddenly I break through the vegetation. The air is fresher up here; the breeze cools my skin, wrapping itself around me as I stand for a moment relishing the feel. Lifting my ponytail, the wind creeps across my neck, drying the sweat that has built up there. I look around; below me the town waits, but from here it is so small, so insignificant. I can see no movement from it, it could be a toy waiting for someone to come and play with it.

The top of the hill is flat and featureless; it takes me a moment to realise I am alone, he is not here. I walk across to the other side of the clearing, the long grass tickling my ankles as it brushes against me; the other side of the hill is dusty and arid, nowhere to hide. I turn, unsure. He can't have just vanished. The grass twitches at my side as something grabs at my ankle and pulls me down; I squeal like a little girl as I tumble down into his arms; pushing him away I sit up embarrassed, turning away so he can't see the flush across my skin. The grass is long, hiding him perfectly in its fronds, the wind blows across it, colours shifting from greens to blues to silver. The grass ebbs and flows in waves as if here, on this apex in the middle of the countryside, is an ocean; I twist my fingers through the grass, letting the blades quiver against my fingertips. I close my eyes: up here I can smell the air, the grass whispers around me, the sound getting closer and closer, the smell getting heavier and stronger, the hairs on my arm stand up in anticipation; I open my eyes as the whole world seems to go quiet. The colours have been leached from the day leaving everything in sepia tones, the first swollen drop of rain explodes against my shoulder, cold against the heat of my skin. The sky churns above, in the distance the clouds are torn apart by a claw of lightning. Aware that the storm is heading our way, he grabs my hand and we race, sliding on the scree as we hasten down the barren windswept side of the hill. Ahead of us a stands a small wooden hut, desolate in its isolation. Usually I would wrinkle my nose up at the thought of going inside the decrepit building, but the rain has already plastered my clothes to me like a second skin and although it looks as if it will collapse under the storms onslaught, there is no other shelter nearby.

We slam the door closed behind us, as the shed creaks in dissension; the rain hammers at the roof looking for a way in. I peel the cooling fabric away from my skin as I look around. The shed is empty, but apart from a bit of dust it's dry and clean.

I pick at my top again, my skin irritated where the damp fabric keeps sticking. Without thinking he takes off his shirt and wipes his hair and face dry. I wish I could do the same, knowing though that what is appropriate for him is not for me, I content myself with picking at the fabric, hoping that the rain will pass soon.

He pulls a pack of cards from his pocket; turning them over we play, wasting time until we are free again. Each card seems to be a portent, turning them over one by one… queen of hearts, ace of spades; each card seems to jump out at me, telling me a story, as if he's reading my fortune with tarot cards. He beats me easily, laughing at my distraction.

A beam of sunlight shines through the grubby window illuminating the pile of cards, dust motes dance in its length as I look up towards it. The shed creaks in the sun's warmth as if it is stretching, the sun streams through every gap in the wood, each knothole glowing red as the shed is transformed from dismal greys to a fire of burnt oranges and warm yellows; baking in the sun, its smells permeate the air, rich and heady and warm. Stepping outside, the smell of the wood is overpowered by the earthy tang of ozone from the storm.

"Petrichor." I mean to only think it, but the word jumps from my mouth. He looks at me in confusion. "The scent of rain on the earth, it's called petrichor." He nods at my babbling and turns away, breathing deeply the fresh scent.

My clothes become stiff as the sun's heat dries them. Itchy and uncomfortable, we head for home with promises to meet later and an agreement to sneak out and camp overnight in the hut.

Turning the key in the lock I call out to my mum – there is no answer. Glad to avoid any awkward questions, I pick up the phone and call her at work.

"Yes I am staying at Jenny's, yes it's okay with her mother." Questions answered, I know I am safe; even if my mum decides to phone and check, Jenny is away, on holiday in France. I shower and change; grabbing my sleeping bag I run back out into the darkening night.

I lie in the darkness. The cold from the floor beneath me seeps through the thin sleeping bag and penetrates my body, making my joints ache. I stretch, the chill making me feel old, as if the inertia of this, of lying here, is aging me, mocking me. *If you will not live and dance and move, I will take your youth and give it to someone who will use it, take pleasure from it, cherish it.* My eyes dart, awake, alert; my body thrums as the muscles want to move, to force this coldness from my body, the sleeping bag feeling less like a protective embrace and more like a shroud. The moon glints through the window, painting everything with a patina of silver, as I glance at him asleep beside me. I know I should sleep, that he will worry if I am not here when he wakes, but the call is too much. Easing myself from my sleeping bag, I can feel each muscle as they stretch, warmth flooding my limbs as the blood starts to flow again causing pins and needles. I stretch my legs, my feet touch the cold concrete floor; wincing I withdraw them quickly, folding them beneath me to warm them with my own body heat while I search for my sneakers. Lacing them I carefully make my way to the door. I glance over my shoulder to see if he has woken – in one way I hope that he has so we can continue to share this day, but a selfish part of me hopes he remains asleep so that this magic time can be for me and only for me. I ease open the door and step out into the night.

Everything is still, as if I have stepped into a picture. The nocturnal creatures have made their way back to their hides and burrows, tucking themselves away from the coming daylight and the hustle and bustle of mankind. Silence, not just quiet but an enveloping absence of sound, that moment of purity before it is shattered by the song of the birds heralding a new day. As I walk across the grass, I feel the dew cool against my ankles, fresh and new, every sensation is exquisite in its isolation. The silver etchings from the moon fade as I walk through the woodland, darkness enveloping me as the sharp lines of black and silver begin to merge into shades of grey. The ground tilts upwards as I make my way towards dawn light, the musky smell of the woodland floor rises up to me on this still night, bark and leaves decaying, bringing life once again to this place. I emerge from the scent and step out towards the top of the hill; sitting, I watch as the lights start to appear below. One by one the glimmers of light seem to eclipse the stars in the sky; as a light is ignited below, one above is extinguished.

Soon the world will be theirs, but for now there is just me, and it is enough.

|The Flood|

~

Steve's back ached, his knees ached, everything ached. The damp air from Innsmouth always managed to get into his joints these days. It had never really bothered him before, living so close, but whether it was down to his age or to the fact that the waters were rising more quickly these days, that damp always seemed to exasperate his arthritis more now.

Steve reached for a box filled with newspapers and magazines, the weight bending him almost in two as he lifted it up, knees bent, back straight. He laughed, a harsh barking noise like a seal, which quickly deteriorated into a liquid burble – the same noise that the sewer water made, now that it ran mere millimetres under the road level. Steve's back hadn't been straight in years. Decades of working down the mines had bent him to the shape of the tunnels, long hours and lack of daylight bowing his bones in his formative years. But there wasn't anyone to help him: the village, the lane, the house, empty except for himself since Sylvie had died. Any neighbours they'd had, had moved out long ago; their children telling tales of bogeymen, of whispers, of lisping entreaties from swollen pond and stream and brook.

Steve missed the sound of the children playing. A maelstrom of noise that crashed and broke wildly as the children discarded their games on the shoreline – castles built in trees rather than of sand – as their games crept ever higher, away from the grasping muddied bog of their gardens. But soon even their frantic shouts and frenzied games ebbed away as their parents pulled them inside, away from the idyllic childhood they'd envisioned for their offspring when they moved here – not questioning why the houses, so quaint, and the village, so picturesque, were so cheap – before, one by one, they left. Their houses crumbled, their facades flaking away in the harsh sea air. Mildewed curtains pulled to hide the patches of mould that crept once more across their freshly painted walls. 'For sale' signs tilting as they sank into the boggy morass that had once been a lush and verdant lawn.

He and Sylvie had never had children. He was pretty sure the problem was him, there were no tests back then of course, or at least not for people like them; there may have been tests for those rich city folk, he didn't know, but the one thing he was pretty sure about was that the problem was with him, with his swimmers, as he put it. He'd told Sylvie she should find someone else, someone that she could have children with, children who could look after her. He'd shrugged and said, "You know, for later on, when I've gone." But Sylvie didn't answer him, just smiled a half smile, tears in her eyes and hugged him. She never did leave him, at least not for children, and by then it didn't matter, she would never have her later on.

Steve stacked the boxes in the spare room. Starting by the window he built a wall. Casting the room in darkness, box by box, brick by brick, he hid the rain that continued to fall outside. *Saint Swithin's day if thou dost rain, for forty days it will remain.* Steve wasn't sure when Saint Swithin's day was, but he was pretty sure that it'd had been raining. It always seemed to rain these days.

Steve placed the armchair at the top of the stairs and slumped into it, staring down at the front door and the door mat that lay in front of it. That and the sofa were the only things that still remained down there. He'd even managed to force the fridge up the stairs, but he wasn't too sure how well that had worked. Something had leaked out from the bottom of it, tracing a slug trail of ichor across the landing that had seeped into the carpet, leaving an odd taint like ozone in the air, but whether it was some chemical from the fridge, or just some stale standing water from the miniscule freezer compartment, he neither knew or cared. By that point his joints were on fire and his muscles were screaming. He no longer gave a shit about the carpet; the whole thing would probably have to come up once the waters got in anyway.

Steve arched his back, the vertebrae fused together, refusing to pop. He knew he should stand and stretch before he seized up, he wasn't a young man anymore, but he could no longer find the energy to move.

Just for a moment. Steve knew he was lying to himself, there wasn't a hope in hell of him moving in a moment, he felt like he could just sit here forever, never moving from the curves of the chair that had moulded over the years to his body, cushions sagging round him now as his skin sagged from his bones, the meat of his body eaten away by age, scraggly and tough like the mutton his parents used to put in the stew pot when he was younger. He could sit here forever but it wouldn't bring him much comfort, his flank too scrawny to hide the lumpy cushion where the springs poked through, pressing against the deadened nerves in his rump and shoulders.

Maybe he would stay here, sleep here. His bed was covered in boxes of junk; keepsakes and knick-knacks that Sylvie had gathered over the years. Items and images that meant so much to her, though he could never see what she saw in them. "Memories" she called them, when she caught him sneering at one of her shells one day, turning the gentle sweep of coral and pearl over in his hand. "Don't sneer like that. Your face will stick like it if the wind changes and you'll end up looking like them over in Innsmouth."

He'd wanted to say he hadn't been sneering, that he'd been peering, trying to understand; but it seemed pedantic to tell her. Now of course he wished he had, that he'd told her that he wasn't laughing at her keepsakes, at her memories, at her; that he was trying to understand them. But of course there are always so many things that we wish we'd said, far more of those words than the ones we wish we hadn't. *If wishes were fishes*, his mum always used to say. He felt so tired.

Staring down the stairs at the door mat he was sure it had changed colour. Just at the edge where it met the door, the sand-coloured nap turning to the rich umber of freshly dug earth. Steve knew he should go down, see if the discolouration was merely shadows or in fact the first encroaching tendrils of flood water seeping past his threshold, but he couldn't be bothered, not anymore. The impetus of earlier had left him, and now he wasn't even sure why he'd bothered to bring everything upstairs. Why he'd been so upset at the thought of the sofa getting damaged – it wasn't as if it needed to be replaced, there was only him to sit down, and he could always just sit in the armchair. Lethargy dragged at his body as he stared down at the mat, his head drooping towards his chest. As sleep finally overtook him, Steve wondered if maybe he should have moved the chair back just a fraction from the top of the stairs.

Crepuscular shadows painted the walls of the landing when Steve woke. Pain emanated from his neck, infiltrating every inch of his body, as if poison rather than blood was being pumped through his veins. He tried to stand, to stretch, but his legs gave way, dropping him back into the chair, his meagre weight inching the chair back slightly but not enough to tip it backwards. Slowly Steve's head cleared from the fug of sleep, his leaden limbs waking, pins and needles prickling over the nerve-deadening throb of his abused muscles. Realising where he was, Steve glanced down the stairs to where the darkness crept up the walls. The mat now a dark swampy grey, the colour of the salt flats where the mine used to pump its waste into the sea when he was a boy.

He couldn't tell in the darkening house if those were just shadows, painted on the wall and flooding across the welcome mat towards the foot of the stairs, or flood water. *Once my legs have some feeling in them, I should go down and check* Steve thought to himself whilst he kneaded the knotted muscles in his thighs, but even as he thought it a hollowness grew in the pit of his stomach. He knew he wouldn't. In the same way he knew he would never say those words out loud, not for fear that someone may overhear and think he'd gone nutty in his old age, but because some*thing* might hear and hold him to his word.

The stench of ozone had grown stronger whilst he slept. In the darkness he could no longer see if the fridge was still leaking, or if instead the smell was emanating from those shadows below. A miasma of sewer and sea and river, all raising, all looking for breaches in his home. Maybe he should have left when the others did. They weren't local to here though, just newcomers attracted to the low house prices, who sent their children to the city for school, rather than down the road to the old, tiny schoolhouse that housed the local villagers' children.

To be fair he wasn't really local himself, a blow in as Sylvie used to say, but he was local enough, born in the next town along, where the house prices were cheap but not as cheap as they were here. Local enough to know that if he and Sylvie had been blessed with children, he too would have insisted on sending them on the bus into the city for school. Local enough to know that leaving didn't necessarily ensure safety, and that once gone there was little hope of there being any return. He was local enough – and old enough – to realise that the idea of starting again from scratch was scarier than anything the floods could bring. So after the first month of rain he'd started to pack. He'd cleared his train set from the guest room and stored it in the attic alongside suitcases of summer clothes that he lugged up and tossed next to the Christmas decorations. After the second month, when the salt flats turned to marsh, he boxed up any non-essentials and stacked them in corners downstairs. Then today – or was it now yesterday – when the river broke its banks and the sea began to creep, he started the back breaking job of lugging his life upstairs, trying to save as much of it as possible.

Steve shifted his chair back from the edge of the stairs, the darkness below growing silently. Steve cocked his head to listen, trying to hear the tell-tale sound of water flooding around the door, but the rain was beating too loudly on the windows and roof to be able to tell if that gentle susurrance that whispered in his ear was the gradual transgression of water, or the sound of distant waves crashing onto the beach. Cautiously he picked his way round his belongings, careful not to knock the stacks over and tip something vital like the coffee machine down the stairs.

Sweeping the wall with his hand, his fingers brushed against the light switch. From below there came a plop. Steve froze, his fingers rigid against the switchplate as he held his breath, waiting for the sound to come again. *Plop*, the noise dissonant within the walls of the house. The only time he had heard that sound before was when he used to go Bass fishing down south, as the fish lay dying, spasming in the hull of the boat. Was it his imagination or was the underlying essence of the smell now more one of disease than chemicals? He flicked the switch and for a second the lights flared on, brightness blinding him, before there was the resonating bang of a fuse blowing, leaving his flare-burned eyes blinder than they had been before.

He knew it was pointless, but still Steve flicked the switch on and off, blinking his eyes in time to the movements, up and down, as he waited for his eyes to recover from the shock of light. "Maybe it's just the bulb." Steve whispered to himself. For a moment he paused flicking the switch. Holding his breath, fear caught in his chest as he wondered what he would do if something in the dark replied to him. *You're a fool, an old man scared by the dark.* He spoke the words in his mind before a final, firm flip turned the light switch to off. But he couldn't bring himself to utter them out loud. Steve reached round the doorway to the bedroom, shutting his eyes and praying. He flipped the switch, but even before he opened his eyes he knew it was to no avail, the shadows remained, deeper, they inched closer, now hiding almost everything. He stepped carefully over the now defunct coffee machine and approached the stairs. Had the waters now reached the bottom step, or was that darkness nothing more than the night?

Steve cursed himself for not thinking to get any candles. The torch was downstairs next to the fuse board in the cellar. But if the water had got in there, what chance did he have of getting the electrics back? He cursed himself again – his microwave meals, his coffee, none of those would do him any good if he didn't have any electric. He just hadn't thought, hadn't realised, of course if the water got in downstairs it'd blow the fuses. *But maybe it isn't the water; it could just be a blown bulb that tripped the system*, the practical voice in his head cut in.

Steve edged his way down the stairs, step by step, gripping on to the handrail. The fetid stench definitely seemed stronger down here, so maybe on the plus side he hadn't knackered the fridge, though what use a fridge without electricity would be he had no idea. *Plop.* The noise echoed the creak of the stair, causing Steve to grip the handrail tighter, as if his hand was trying to prevent his descent. *There's water to drink upstairs, crackers to eat, a loo, a chair, a bed. You'll be better to check in the morning, otherwise you'll just end up breaking your fool neck.*

Steve's hand tightened once more on the bannister, causing it to creak beneath his hand. From below came an answering *plop, plop, plop* as if someone had just thrown a bucketful of tiddlers back into a lake.

Steve licked at his parched lips; he'd eaten some crackers, but when he went to grab a glass of water, the smell from the sink made him retch. There was some milk in the fridge but not much, he took a sip, still cool – he knew he should ration it out, but it wouldn't keep long with the power out. He took another sip before putting it back away and closing the door, hoping that the seal would keep it cool at least for a while.

He needed a pee. The smell when he opened the bathroom door hit him like a wave, brackish; the room felt damp, dank, the rain hammered against the window like nails as the wind changed direction. Slamming the toilet seat down, Steve peed in the bath before thrusting the plug in. Urine pooling against his hand, he flicked it into the sink before firmly pressing that plug in place too, wiping his hand on the towel to dry it, before pulling the door shut. Edging his way back to the stairs, Steve collapsed into the armchair and watched as the darkness crept ever closer.

Steve realised he must have dozed off, as the speckled light on the walls had turned grey. The rain on the windows made it look as if the paint on the walls had dripped and run. The light also showed Steve that he'd been right – overnight the water had broken past the barrier of his door and had edged up the stairs, already covering the first three steps, leaving only ten more till it reached the landing where he sat.

The water lapped gently against the balustrades, ripples eddying round the circular posts. Steve wasn't sure what he'd expected, but he hadn't expected it to be this quick, and he certainly hadn't expected it to be this *clean*. He thought flood water would be brown and stink of the sewers as they all flowed into one, but the water beneath, other than being a little silty, looked clean, and the smell was more reminiscent of the harbour where he went fishing when he holidayed down south, than the smell of the toilets when they backed up.

Plop. Ripples fanned out from the doorway, one of the glass panels was cracked and another appeared to have gone completely. *It must have been the sound of the glass dropping*. It'd be fine. Easy enough to fit a new door once this was all over. Light shimmered on the waters down the end of the hall, ripples fanning back across the length of the hallway. *Plop*. Steve whipped his head back, causing his muscles to twinge in response. Rubbing his neck, Steve peered at the doorway.

The crack hadn't grown and he couldn't see any other missing panes of glass. *Maybe it was one of the ones underwater.* Steve worked at the knot of pain that was threatening to spread down his arm, and tried to ignore the voice in his head that pointed out that he wouldn't have heard the plop of water if it had fallen beneath the surface.

The water had reached the seventh step by the time he'd run out of milk. He'd drunk it relatively quickly to be fair, remembering the scotch that was packed into one of the boxes in the bedroom. And he couldn't be blamed for sipping at the scotch if that was all he had left.

By the time the waters reached the tenth step, the door was submerged and the steady *plop, plop, plop* had mercifully ceased, though the waters churned like a maelstrom. Shadows darting within, curling around themselves. Their darkness shimmering silver, as they swam through the lighter waters where the door used to be. The water roiling as they thrashed, propelling themselves swiftly away, back towards the darker waters which inched closer and closer to the landing.

By the time the waters reached the thirteenth step and started to ebb and flow along the landing, the bottle of scotch was empty. Steve tried to lift his feet, to curl them foetally into himself on the chair, but whether it was the time he'd spent sitting watching the eddies of water, or whether it was the scotch taking effect, his feet wouldn't obey. His only ability was to wiggle his toes, and even that seemed to dissipate as the frigid waters soaked through his slippers, and the waters – well, he hoped it was the waters – lapped against his ankles.

For the first time ever Steve was glad that Sylvie had passed and that they'd never managed to have children. Because his neighbours over at Innsmouth had children, and he was pretty sure they weren't here to play.

|The Final Cut|

~

Our mothers thought it hilarious when they found out that, as well as being in neighbouring hospital beds, they lived in neighbouring houses. They lay there, wincing, as laughter tugged painfully at their wounds. My mother obviously found this funnier than Tim's, as her laughter ripped her stitches apart one by one. I wonder if my mother envied Tim's. Whether she watched, green eyes wide, as Tim's mother sunbathed in the garden, that delicate silver line etched across the top of her bikini, while my mother sat swaddled in a kaftan to cover the red, puckered wound across her torso. Did my mother envy that first incision; that skin cut neater, the stitches tighter?

Tim always got the best, right from the start. My mother told me stories about how that first summer they'd sit in the garden feeding us, as our fathers ripped down the fence that ran across the back of our houses. My father blushing and averting his eyes from the nipple that would pop out of Tim's mouth once he was sated; my mother bottle feeding me as I wouldn't latch. I wonder if even then I had stared enviously at him, nestling snugly against the warmth of the breast, as I bit into my silicone teat.

Our childhoods are recounted often by our mothers, a wistful remembrance shared with anyone who'll listen. An Enid Blyton tale illustrated with thousands of faded photos. There we are lying on a gingham blanket at our mothers' feet as they sewed our first teddy bears – still sitting pride of place, propped against pillows on our childhood beds, waiting for the time when grandchildren will fill their houses – that was the first time I felt it, that envy growing inside me; those first tendrils, twisting in my gut. Our mothers had worked all summer to make those bears. Maybe it was because Tim's mother's fingers were nimbler, or because my mother's were numbed due to the cocktail of painkillers she still took for her inflamed wound, that

Tim's bear came out perfect, plump and plush; the material cut neater, the stitches tighter. Whereas mine sagged, the stuffing leaking from its seams.

As the summer sun turned to winter rain, our mothers moved their sewing inside. Each house was set up with two of everything: two sewing boxes, two sets of shears, two seam rippers. They revelled in the absurdity of it. Laughing on our first day at playschool when the other parents enquired whether we were twins, dressed as we were in identical blue romper suits – the children laughed too, when my pants split during a game of leap frog. Or on our first day at school where there was no polyester uniform from Asda for us – Tim's uniform smart and pressed, the cut neater, the stitches tighter; whilst mine sagged, the hem of my trousers coming undone before the final bell of the day.

As we grew, our mothers insisted we did everything together: birthdays, Christmases, holidays. Though I drew the line at getting married on the same day. I wasn't sharing my fiancée, Jennifer, with anyone. My mother pouted and pleaded, told me it was more economical, hinted that there'd be money for a honeymoon. She finally conceded when I agreed she could make the wedding dress.

Our weddings were a week apart, and whilst Tim's bride looked radiant in white, her dress cut neater, the stitches tighter, Jennifer looked like a deflated sail.

Our wives started sewing once Tim announced the pregnancy. Pastel blanket squares. Jennifer dropped hints as she sewed, each cut neat, the stitches tight. Unbeknownst to her, I'd had one of my colleagues give me the snip straight out of medical school. There'd be no surrogate sibling.

The blankets grew, as did Tim's wife. Jennifer took hers everywhere, draping it over her lap during the day, hugging it to her stomach at night. It took me weeks to realise that it wasn't for the comfort, but for the occultation that she clung to it. I was as ignorant of her growth as I was of the furtive glances between the two of them.

Well, tonight I've brought my surgeon's kit home, and unlike my mother's, my cuts are neat, my stitches tight.

|Warpaint|

"Please." My girlfriend Katie snaked her arms round my middle. "It'll be fun. I'll let you *take* me on the tunnel of love." She winked lasciviously. "It's only here for one more night. Pleeeeeease John. Pretty please with sugar on top."

"I…I can't. Why don't you go with Jodie?"

Katie pouted as she moved away to pour herself her morning coffee. "Can't. She's loved up with her new man. Anyway, they've already been. Everyone's already been, except me. Come on. I love the carnival. Don't you?"

I didn't, I hated them; had done ever since my parents had taken me to my one and only carnival when I was a kid. Even the smell of fried onions at a diner made me queasy, triggering a Pavlovian response, the smell like brimstone as I thought back to that hellish night.

I gripped my mother's hand tight as they dragged me through the gates towards the sounds of sirens and screams. Lights strobing in the darkening sky made the shadows that lurked around the edges of the booths pulse. Huge grotesque faces on the hoardings above the rides leered and winked at me as I hurried past, their paint scabbed and peeling beneath the harsh neon glow. The whole thing made me want to cry along with the screams that echoed through the midway. I tightened my grip on my mother's hand and she looked down at me, laughter crinkling her eyes.

"Having fun?"

I nodded. As young as I was, I noticed that her eyes hadn't crinkled like that for a long time.

"Course he is." My dad ruffled my hair and I stiffened, fought against the compulsion to pull away. It was unusual for my dad to touch me; it felt odd, weird. I don't think I ever remember him touching me before, though he must have done. Mom keeps a photo of him cradling me on the day I was born, in pride of place on the television. At night, before bed, I always looked at that photo. It started as a way to say goodnight to him when he wasn't home. Mom used to sit me on her lap and read me a story as I drank my hot chocolate. Then, once I'd finished it, she'd tell me to say night to Daddy. One night I refused. Whether it was because I didn't want to go to bed, or because I'd said night to a photo more often than I had my dad, I can't remember, but my mom just sat there, her lips tight. I thought she was going to tell me off, force me to say it, but instead she just nodded once, then read me another story from my book.

So even though I wasn't having fun at the carnival, I didn't pull away. I'd have done anything to keep that smile on my mom's face. So I just nodded under my father's hand and gripped my mom's all the more tightly.

It was late by the time I pulled up to the house. I'd checked every file at work twice before sending them off, and had been about to check the next day's workload as my phone beeped with the message *Where R U?*

I flipped the phone over so it was screen down and tried to refocus on the tasks that beckoned to me from the computer screen on my desk. The monitor's illumination was the only sign of life in the dark office space, until the stark overhead lights hummed into life.

"Shit!" screamed the cleaner.

My chest hitched, the responding scream cut off, my intake of breath masked by the clattering sound of a mop being dropped.

"S'cuse my language. I didn't think anyone was still here."

I waved away her apology as I reluctantly shut down my computer to head home before she started to vacuum under my feet.

The rain soaked me as soon as I stepped out into the parking lot, my anxiety washing away with it. Hidden away in the high rise, I'd been unaware of the change in weather. It felt as if a huge burden had been shifted from my shoulders to be replaced by the heavy, rain-sodden material of my jacket. In seconds I was drenched, the water leaching through the heavy weave and saturating my shirt beneath, the chill a welcome shock after the heavy heat inside.

A weight lifted from my chest as I made my way home; there was no way Katie would want to go out in this. I pulled over at a pizza joint, its windows emblazoned with lurid carnival posters. I ordered – making sure to keep my eyes averted from the gurning clowns that grinned at me from the window – then headed next door to grab some flowers as an apology for working late and missing Katie's text.

I browsed the bottles of wine on offer whilst I counted down the minutes until I could pick up the pizza. The idea of that grinning face on the poster – its swollen lips, red, slashed into a mean smile which reached across its face – watching me whilst I waited for my dinner to cook turned my stomach. Then I heard it: a high pitched, humming tone.

I put down the wine I was holding and cocked my head, trying to tell where the noise was coming from. Was it behind me, out in front towards the door, above in the heating ducts? I was heading towards the end of the aisle when the humming started to roll, and the sound became akin to a voice, singing, high like a child's but not so sweet. With a growl hidden away at the back, like the sound of someone who'd smoked forty a day and drunk whisky for breakfast. The sound started to undulate. I was still heading towards it, head forward and cocked to the side as I concentrated, trying to isolate the song from the other noises of the store. It was frustrating how the beeps of the till and the shush of the meat slicer at the deli counter layered on top of the humming, obscuring the song. I made my way closer, edging towards it, trying to figure it out, following the juvenile tune without looking too much like a freak, or a paedo following a kid round the store. Then suddenly the humming broke into a discordant jumble of syllables, lungs far bigger than any child's should be shrieking out *Do, do, doodle oddle, do, do, do, do...* The song's name eluded me, something to do with storms and fire, with fighters and entrances. But even if my brain couldn't remember what the song was, my body did. It was always about entrances, about things sneaking in, hidden behind make up and prosthetics and masks; about things concealed behind bleachers and within cars; about gaudily painted boxes with tiny handles designed for tiny hands to turn and produce a teeny-tiny tinny version of that discordant, frivolous melody, to bewitch them with the music that their little hands had never before made, then *POP!*

I rushed back down the aisle, away from the frenzied chanting, exiting through the entrance doors as someone stepped through from outside. It wasn't until I was back in the greasy warmth of the pizza shop that I realised I was still clutching the bunch of flowers tightly in my fist.

The light was on, silhouetting Katie's slender figure in the living room. Her face periodically lit up from below as she glanced down at the phone in her hand, the light painting her face white. Dark shadows pooled in her eyes, as the rain ran down the window pane, and coursed down her cheeks, gouging rivulets into her flesh that flowed with dark tears. The car stank of grease and funeral homes, thanks to the cooling pizza and the wilting flowers, as I sat there a moment watching her, until impatience flashed across her face and she disappeared from view, the front door opening before I had even turned off the engine.

"Hope you've already eaten. If not, you'll have to grab something there."

I'd not even stepped through the door before Katie was slipping her coat on, her hand already reaching for her bag as I tried to juggle my car keys, the door, her flowers, and tonight's pizza. I didn't understand what she was talking about so I simply said, "I've bought us pizza. Sorry I'm late. I was stuck in a meeting."

Katie took the proffered flowers and pizza box and headed into the kitchen. I'd just slipped a shoe off as I heard her say, "We can heat it up later. When we get back."

"Back? From where?" I hoped that I'd managed to make my tone innocently questioning, but even to my ear it sounded querulous and nervous.

"The carnival. It's the last night. I was hoping to have a bit more time there but we can always stay late."

"But it's pissing it down! And I've got an early start." I could hear the whine in my voice, and hated myself for it. Tears pricked my eyes and I blinked rapidly, trying to hold them back; I didn't want Katie to see me cry. My heart thumped in time with my blinks, my head swam as Katie's voice echoed down the hallway.

"When did you get so old? Come on, grumpy, it'll be fun. They've got clowns." Katie's voice crept up at the end of the sentence as if she was trying to tempt a toddler with an ice cream. I opened my mouth to answer, but by that point Katie must have realised that something was wrong because she stepped towards me, frowning. She reached out as if to embrace me as I tumbled forwards, the whole world flipping, a kaleidoscope of colours bursting in front of my eyes before everything went black.

"Come on, son, don't be a grump, you'll have fun. They've got clowns." My father's voice sounded odd; it wasn't just that I wasn't used to him talking to me, it was that the tone he was using didn't quite match his features. The words rolled in a jovial manner, sounds bouncing up and down in a melody of speech, but his tone was clipped, a calliope of notes which matched the rigour of his face.

My arm ached as he pulled me across the uneven scrub, hassocks of grass protruding from the hard ground that my feet bumped and twisted along as he dragged me towards the tent at the end of the midway. The big top engulfed the end of the carnival. I peeked back over my shoulder, checking that mom was still with us and hadn't been eaten by the crowds. She was way back, laughing, her arm cocked back, a ball in her hand. A young man held her close, her hand in his; he brought their arms back then swiftly forward, a crash of cans, a scream that could have been either joy or fear, as the hawker pulled my mother towards the back of the stall. I tugged at my father's arm to get him to turn back, to get my mom, but the only response was a hard yank straight up.

Red pain lanced through my shoulder, causing me to twist back to alleviate the pressure before my arm popped out of its socket. Once my father had lowered his arm, and I'd fallen back in step with him, I glanced back along the midway. The arched entrance shone like a faraway beacon, its light fanning out towards the food trucks and games that lined the main thoroughfare. Mom stood alone, spot-lit under the stall's neon lights, her arm held out in front of her, her hand cut off by the shadows that hid the interior of the stall and its inhabitants from me. She stepped forward, her arm now amputated at the elbow. My mouth opened and closed silently, like those of the goldfish that hung in bags alongside the candyfloss and rainbow coloured candy corn. My mind screamed *No*, as I twisted round. The pain in my shoulder flared at the exact same moment that my mom took another step and the awning's shadow reached her shoulder.

My foot slid into a divot, twisting me round so that the pain in my shoulder arched across my back. A corresponding grunt came from my father before he let go of my hand and I tumbled onto the dusty floor. Tears blurred my vision. I swiped at my eyes, dirt from my gritty hands painting my face. When I looked back, my mother was gone, and another woman stood under the neon lights where she'd once been.

My father stood there, his arms folded, as I blurted out my warning. My goldfish-like silence burst as the words poured out, a torrent of disjointed sentences that washed over my father as he stood there tapping his foot.

I woke to the clammy touch of a wet flannel against my forehead. The floor was hard against my body but my head was cushioned at an awkward angle by something. I reached up and felt my rucksack there, my lunch box digging into my neck.

"Are you okay?" A glass of water was thrust against my lips, the rim clipping my teeth, water spilling down my front as I gasped, attempting to swallow the ice cold liquid before it drowned me. I nodded, causing water to trickle into my ears.

"What happened? Are you still okay to go out?"

Tears pricked my eyes as I shook my head. Placing the glass on the sideboard next to her keys, Katie sat back on her haunches, her face pale beneath her foundation.

"What is it? Are you unwell?"

I shook my head. "It's the carnival."

The video shone luridly from Katie's tablet. The clown's hand lifted, obscuring the painted face on the screen, before it quickly swiped down. The loose skin sagged, tugged down so that the eye drooped and the mouth was pulled into a snarl, before the hand lifted and the skin sprang back into place. The face stared back at me, half masked, half stripped bare. The eyes and the mouth on the left side seemed small and piggy compared to the swollen painted obscenity on the right.

"See? There's nothing to be frightened of."

The clown continued to remove the heavy greasepaint from its face, cloths stained red piling up in front of him as he wiped away the final vestiges of his bloated smile. Lotion turned the blue and black that ringed his eyes into a painted bruise that he wiped clean before tossing the cloth atop the sanguine pile in front of him.

"See? It's just make-up. They're just normal people like you and me."

The face smiled at me, naked, skin pink as a baby's where the cloths had removed every trace of the greasepaint. The man stared back at me; he could have been anything or anyone now: a banker, a bus driver, a solicitor, or a street sweeper.

"I'll stick the kettle on." Katie's hand squeezed my knee reassuringly before she stood and made her way into the kitchen. "I'll just pop the pizza into the oven to heat through, too."

The face on the screen continued to smile, before turning slowly to the left then the right. The video stopped, the image paused, its face turned towards the thumbnail images of people lined up at the side of the screen, waiting for their turn in the spotlight. Clowns stared at me from the screen, frozen, some dour, some grinning; one had its hand raised, whether in greeting or threat was unknown until someone clicked on their image and set the video playing. The bottom thumbnail didn't show a clown; instead, a woman sat turned away from the camera, her long blond hair obscuring the majority of her face. I clicked on it. An advert blared through the speakers of the tablet, before being replaced by the smiling face of my girlfriend as she held up a lipstick and smiled blankly into the camera.

The only time my father hit me was when I mentioned the clowns. He'd deliver a short, sharp slap that burned my face. "Don't be stupid.

That painted bitch left us, that's all. Ran off with some chump from work." That was the only time he spoke of my mom. Even back then I knew she hadn't run off. I'd seen the carnival swallow her whole. If it had just been my father she was leaving behind, than I might have understood. There were many times I ran away from him myself over the years; the final time when I escaped to college, after which I never returned until his funeral. But there was no way my mom would have left me; she loved me. It was the clowns that took her away.

I was at the traffic lights when I first noticed them, sitting in the car alongside mine. They were pouting into their rear-view mirror as they painted their lips as red as the traffic light ahead. They turned and blew me a kiss as the lights turned green before speeding away, their painted faces flashing past me as the horns blared out from the cars behind me.

The next one was introduced to me by my boss as Becky, the new intern. Her swollen bee-stung pout transformed into a Cheshire cat grin that split her face from ear to ear as she held out a hand in greeting. Her knife-sharp nails were the clotted-red colour of blood as her hand enveloped mine, pumping it once, twice. The force aggravating my old shoulder injury, pain flaring in it once more.

Soon, I could see them everywhere – their tattooed faces, their painted grins, their faces frozen into perpetual visages of shock and surprise beneath their jovial masks. An infestation – the woman running down the street with a stumbling, crying child in tow; the barista who served me coffee each morning with a friendly hello; the attendant at the petrol station; the contracts manager; the cleaner. By ten o'clock, I knocked on my boss' door, my head pounding in time to my heart, my breath ragged, sweat beading my hairline and sticking my shirt to my back. As I made my way in, I mumbled, "I'm sorry, I'm not feeling well, it must be something I ate."

My boss looked up, her face masked, unreadable behind the makeup that caked her skin.

"I…I…I need to go home." The room started to swim in front of me as my boss nodded, cracks appearing at the corners of her mouth as her lips opened. I watched, my eyes as wide, as that dark maw opened wider, a black hole that seemed to suck all the air out of the room. I needed to get out of there before I suffocated, before I passed out and she swallowed me whole, but my feet were rooted to the floor.

"Are you okay? You look dreadful. Do you want me to get you anything?"

My paralysis broke as the monster which I'd once mistaken for my boss stood up from behind their desk. "No. No, that's fine. I just need to go."

The monster nodded once. Her eyes tracked my escape, never once looking away or blinking those spindly, spider-leg lashes until the lift doors closed to ferry me to safety.

The road was empty when I pulled up to the house, my journey home largely uneventful now the majority of people were either at work or school. The only people visible were either in the park or hidden away under the shadows of the shop awnings. Too far away for me to tell if they were clowns or normal people like me.

After scurrying up the path, I locked the front door behind me. Thankful for the security of home, I felt my breathing slow, the thumping and tightness in my chest alleviating as I loosened my tie and undid the top button of my shirt. Sweat greased my back as I shrugged the rucksack from my aching shoulder. A hot shower was what I needed. Checking the door was locked once more, I head up the stairs to the bathroom.

The bottle was hidden away behind the shower gel. *"Get that all-natural sun kissed glow in minutes."* I turned the innocuous bottle over in my hand; a brown scum rimmed the cap, painting a line the colour of shit on my palm. I tried to rub it away, but the line remained, a scar across my hand. I thrust the bottle back behind the others on the shower caddy and scrubbed shower gel into my palm until the redness of my skin hid the orange tinge beneath. After that I shut the shower off.

As I dried myself, my eyes swept over all the bottles and jars that cluttered each surface. The only ones that were mine were a can of shaving foam and one of deodorant; all the rest were Katie's, a myriad of bottles and tubes and pots. They were clustered on shelves and stacked on the window sill; a tube of mascara lay cracked on the vanity unit, black ichor gluing it to the surface. The air was heavy with the sickly sweet smell of wax and powder, a chemical undertone that caused my gorge to rise as I staggered into our bedroom. The dressing table, too, was adorned with glass bottles sparkling in the sunlight, a pot of cream positioned next to the alarm clock.

Dressing quickly, I made my way downstairs and grabbed Katie's tablet, clicking on the browser icon to bring up last night's search. Images of clowns stared at me, their faces frozen into grotesque parodies of humanity as they gurned and winked lasciviously from the screen. I clicked on the thumbnail at the bottom which held the image of Katie. The same video as before sprang up on the screen, but my eyes were drawn to the right, away from the sight of my girlfriend lining and painting her face. I scrolled down through the images, each one was Katie. Katie holding a lipstick, a brush, her face naked and blank staring through the bristles directly at me.

Carefully, I placed the tablet back where it came from. Calmness settled over me, dampening my fear. My father hadn't wanted to tell me the truth about my mother, but I'd been a child then, weak. I made my way into the kitchen and opened the knife draw. I checked my watch; Katie would be home from work soon. I smiled at my reflection in the knife's blade. She'd tell me the truth; there'd be no more hiding behind a mask of lies.

|To Pray at Your Temple|

She danced like no one was watching. The lights slick as they bathed her body in violet and blue, a settling bruise that twisted and spun in time to the music, or at least to the music that played in her head. An adipocere of sweat gathered in the hollows of her neck, clavicles imprisoning the neon lights, a penumbral necklace that cojoined and snaked its way down between her meagre breasts. Saying a prayer to Saint Vitus, she shook off the shackles they tied her down with. Raising skeletal arms she devoted herself to the litany. Stigmata encircling her at the wrist and ankle, a memento, a remembrance of those left behind, of those held in beds, and chairs, and arms. Of those not allowed this dance.

In the beginning they called us vain, as we averted our eyes from the very image of ourselves.

Then they called us wanton, as we swathed ourselves in habit and mantle.

They called us histrionic, as we kept our heads down at our father's table.

Before finally they called us ill.

There was to be no supplication to our gods here, no devotions made to our saints, to Jerome, to Catherine de Siena, or Rosa de Lima. Instead we're told to put our faith in Aesculapius, in Aceso and Aegle. That our enlightenment is only possible, if we turn our backs on our old beliefs and give ourselves completely to their new faith. Though I do not know why they would covet our conversion, we are unsuitable as acolytes; unwilling to take communion, unable to find meaning in their words. They say we are blind to the truth, our perceptions as warped as our bodies, as we sit, heads bowed, waiting for them to leave so we can find meaning in their silence, truth in their echoes, solace in the quiet they leave in their wake.

There were many of us there in those hallowed halls, those unbelievers hollowed in stomach and spirit. For most of us, we had taken up our vows, our tears hushed, our prayers whispered to deities that we dared not address, except in secret. Though occasionally those gods of Paean would trip up, and the heretic that stumbled through those doors would not be broken, would not have retreated fearfully inside the withered husk of their body. But instead would call upon us to worship at their temple, to gaze upon their sharp angles, to lay our hands upon their fragile skin, to understand the message that they brought to us within that desiccated parchment. They did not come quietly, with muted liturgies hidden behind cracked lips and parched tongues. They came shouting and screaming, speaking in tongues that no one understood, a glossology of threats and curses and promises.

It was due to the sacrifice of one of these martyrs that I finally managed to escape those sainted halls. As they lay upon the ground that their feet had worn twisted paths along, crucified by attendants who held them still as their skin was pinched and prepped, pierced by angels who swoop down, waiting for them to quiet, to lay in peace, to sleep. So they could bind their feet, calloused and blistered from the miles they walked within their miniscule cell, their penance. An attrition which even when they removed those martyrs' shoes they couldn't stop.

When all the eyes were upon the fallen, I slipped away, a shadow, staying close to those who had come to visit, the mothers, the fathers, the lovers, the enemies. Hiding my bare feet and unorthodox clothes amongst those who had dressed for outside, for normality, for the world. I escaped amongst the fug of smoke that masked the doorway, ash and embers my shoes, holding my head aloft – my only disguise – I looked ahead.

∾

I returned to where it first began. To that time when I stood erect and elegant, poised and pointed as my body melted to the music. Where my limbs were twisted. Where my feet and torso were bound in silk and bone until I shone above the polished ground. I thought I was beautiful then as I waited in repose, as their hands grasped and their fingers gripped, as they lifted and turned me, an awkward pirouette, as I straightened and folded, as their voices cut me deep: *Too limp, too round, too soft…* Their words hardened me, made me slice away at the layers that held me back.

Now I have returned again to dance for them. The music plays, a jarring of notes, of hard accents, sharp and precise. I turn to face them, their judgement masked by the discordance of the notes. I dance for them. I dance for me. I dance for those who I left behind. I dance until my feet are shod in sanguine slippers, until my skin is swathed in sweat and my peardrop-sweet breath is cut short. I dance my dance, and my dance is sublime.

|The Lepidopterist|

~

Lesson 1: Monday 6th May 2019, 19:58

You learn quite quickly which ones to catch. Those that are curled up in the dark, hidden in corners, layers of clothes cocooning their bodies. Those are the easiest to snare. Of course you will be attracted to the bright colours of those that flit from place to place, sipping on nectar. Their elegant bodies and beauty surpassing those that hide away in the shadowy corners. But theirs is a fragile beauty, so much of it reliant on external factors. And once you capture them their beauty quickly fades, tearing at the slightest touch, their colours soon dull and dissipate until they are more reminiscent of a moth than the butterfly you thought you had captured.

Once you have your specimen it is important to prepare it correctly. The first step is to relax them – I find that alcohol works fine for this initial stage, though for the most skittish you may have to add a little something to the mix. Once you have them relaxed, it should be a synch to get them out and back to where you are intending to display them. I unfortunately only have space for a small collection, so have a tendency to dispose of specimens once they start to fade. Others may only capture them one at a time to study, and certainly for those of you starting out in this field I would suggest only capturing one at a time, you can always dispose of it if you mess up, and it's important to learn and perfect the basics of lepidopterology before you embark on a full collection.

The next step is the most crucial, it is the pinning. I have my own special set up that I developed myself, an old epi-pen device – it protects me from pricking myself with the needle, but you can use any basic hypodermic for this step – that I fill with a special concoction a fellow collector up at the hospital gives me. If possible, I prefer to complete the pinning at home as it can take a little while for the tranquiliser to take full effect. If you do need to complete this step away from where you are spreading the specimen, then as long as you are away from distractions and bright lights you should be fine. Some lepidopterists prefer to avoid the pinning stage completely and instead use Rohypnol or GHB during the relaxing stage. I personally don't recommend the use of illegal drugs in lepidopterology, the people who would sell you these so called "date rape drugs" tend to be quite untrustworthy, and you have no guarantee of the safety or efficacy of the drug that you are administering. There have been many cases of specimens dying before spreading has occurred – always a risk, but the incidences are much higher with the use of date rape drugs over the traditional method of pinning – and worse there have been incidences of the specimens escaping before they have been confined.

The third step is spreading. Now as long as you've followed the first two steps correctly this step is a doddle. There are many ways to spread your specimen, and I suggest experimenting with different forms until you find one that is most aesthetically pleasing for yourself – though remember if you do find one that you find exceptionally appealing, don't restrict yourself to this form for all future specimens; you will often find that what was unpleasing to the eye for one, will be exquisite in another. Once you have the specimen spread to your liking make sure that it is adequately secured in that position. Remember that your specimens are very fragile, and you want to keep them looking their best. Any movement during the next step can lead to dislocation and even breakage of the specimen's limbs.

The fourth and final step is mounting. Now I don't share how I personally go ahead with this step. As was explained in the terms and conditions when you signed up for this course, I believe that this stage is personal and as such is unique to each and every lepidopterist. Most of you will already have experience of this stage anyway, but for those of you who are completely new to the whole process, part of the fun of lepidopterology is in developing your own style. No one is judging you. No one is going to see your collection except for yourself. So, allow yourself the freedom to experiment until you find a mounting system that works for you. Remember we've all had a first time. Lepidopterology is supposed to be fun not a chore.

Now you should all have received a link in your emails that I sent out last night, if you haven't please check that it hasn't gone straight into your spam or junk folder. I am going hunting tonight and will post a video on to that link detailing steps 1 – 3. Again please be aware that I will not be videoing step 4, but if you wish to observe the mounting stage there are plenty of internet sites available that cover that stage. The video will go live tomorrow morning at 10.00am and will stay up for 24 hours after which it will be deleted. Please make sure you do watch the video as we will be discussing it at our next coaching session which will be on Sunday at 10.00am.

∽

Lesson 2: Sunday 12ᵗʰ May 2019, 10:03

As you will all be aware by now there was an issue during the spreading stage with my latest acquisition. I became aware, once I got my specimen home, that unfortunately it was flawed and had excess damage to its front side. Never one to waste a teaching opportunity I decided that the specimen could still be of some use, if the spreading occurred face down. Now unfortunately, whether it was due to some underlying issues with the healthiness of the specimen or whether there was a reaction in the pinning stage, the face down spreading resulted in the death of the specimen due to asphyxiation. This can be quite common, as the usage of alcohol, tranquilisers and the prone position can lead to constriction of the airway, or of the specimen swallowing their own tongue or choking on their own effluence. So instead of today's session covering the stages running up to the mounting of your specimen, we are instead going to focus on what to do if your specimen is deceased. DO NOT WORRY. You will not be missing out on any part of the course, we will just swap the sessions over and we *will* fully cover relaxing, pinning and spreading later in the course. Now most of you will know that in mainstream lepidopterology it is usual for the specimen to be deceased at the point of mounting. Now there are some die hard (no pun intended) purists who insist that as a society we should continue to mount our specimens in this manner; however, that off shoot of lepidopterology is not recognised as being part of the lepidopterology society and the act of mounting the deceased is frowned upon by most lepidopterists today. As I've said before there is no judgement here, but please be aware that it is a requirement of the society that disposal of dead specimens is included in the course content, and if you are intending on mounting the dead this is not a subject we will be discussing either in or out of these sessions. If you wish to find out more information on mounting the deceased there are plenty of internet sites available that cover that particular inclination.

Now my preferred method of disposal is the acid bath. It isn't suitable for all, but it is a good and efficient way of disposing of dead specimens if you have the space. I will be covering other options, dependant on your own circumstances, in your 1:1's. Now it can smell a bit, so I only suggest using this method if you have a lot of land as you will need to position the body so that the smell of the decomposition isn't offensive to the general public. Luckily I live on a farm so if anyone happens upon my land before the disposal is complete, I can blame it on the silage. I have sent you all a link to a live stream. I will start the disposal of the body at 10.00am tomorrow. Could people let me know ASAP if they have an issue with that time, as the first hour of the disposal is the most important. The whole process will take approximately three days, and I will check in with you all at 10.00am on each day to answer any questions you may have.

Lesson 3: Monday 13th May 2019, 10:01

Now it doesn't really matter how large your collection is, you will always need to take into account the correct means of disposal for your specimens. Even your brightest and most beautiful specimen can lose its brilliance over the months and years. And no matter how rich you are, or how big a space you have for storing your collection, you will get to the stage where maintaining a specimen becomes more hassle than it's worth. In the past people have just allowed specimens to go free, or have dumped their bodies as if they are nothing more than rubbish left out for the bin men to collect. This behaviour is not acceptable in the society. You should always treat your specimens with the reverence that they deserve, no matter which stage of the process they are at. Allowing them to go free, or dumping their carcasses as if they were common murder victims, also puts each member of the society at risk, and we have strict procedures on how to deal with members who break this rule.

As I told you yesterday my preferred disposal method is the acid bath. It isn't quick, but it is simple, and I use any leftover product to fertilise my farmland. Now the first step is to get the specimen into the bath, it is important that you remember to put the specimen in before the acid. There are several members who have received quite nasty burns from forgetting and popping the body in after the acid. Now my bath as you can see isn't really a bath it's a trough, an old one that my pigs used to use; if you are using a bath, don't use the one in your bathroom – this isn't smell-o-vision, but just believe me when I say this isn't a smell that you can cover up with an air freshener – and please don't try to flush the waste down the sewers. You'll end up with a blockage and the society's insurance doesn't cover the call out charge for a plumber.

Now I always use a metal plug rather than a rubber one to ensure that the seal doesn't erode whilst the specimen is in the bath. My trough comes fitted with a good heavy duty one that I've attached to a sturdy chain. If you are using the plughole to get rid of the waste product, make sure that you attach a good length of chain to the plug, like this, to aid removal once the process is complete. Once we are happy that the bath is completely sealed we can pour the acid over the specimen. Don't worry if it doesn't cover it completely, we can always give it a poke down when we come back tomorrow; think of it like spaghetti in a saucepan.

～

Lesson 4: Tuesday 14ᵗʰ May 2019, 10:01

As you can see I have opened the door on the barn to allow ventilation. It is unlikely that any animal will be attracted to the smell and just wander in if you don't keep the acid bath somewhere secure. But you don't want to risk any animals injuring themselves or upsetting the delicate procedure. So I tend to keep the barn door locked, and just open it an hour before I do my checks, making sure that I keep the barn in eyesight at all times. I tend to use this time to do an hour's yoga, or to catch up on my emails. Now you don't need anything fancy for this bit of the procedure. I just use an old stick that I used to stir paint when I was decorating my lounge. The most important thing is just to make sure that any parts of the specimen that are still sticking out of the acid are pushed under. If you still have any protuberances – which can happen if your specimen was particularly tall or large – this is the time to add in some more acid.

~

Lesson 5: Wednesday 15ᵗʰ May 2019, 10:03

Usually at this stage in the disposal process, you would be able to see that the bath would be full of a thick, pinkish goo – I always think it looks a lot like the blancmange my Nan used to make for Sunday tea. That pink goo is what is left of the skin, muscles and guts of the specimen. There would usually still be the odd lump left, and some of the larger bones you will struggle to break down unless you grind them down afterwards. However I am unable to show you what your bathtub should look like after 48 hours, as what it shouldn't look like is this. There appears to have been some kind of chemical reaction which has resulted in a hardening of the surface of the acid, forming a kind of carapace which has fused with the bath. I will speak to others within the society for advice regarding this anomaly, and will also send you all out a link to one of my older disposals so you can see how the specimen should be presenting.

~

Lesson 6: Thursday 16ᵗʰ May 2019, 10:27

Apologies for my dishevelled state. I was woken several times during the night by the alarm system in the barn. I have a motion sensor set up inside in case of intruders, but it can be a bit sensitive and occasionally birds or bats get in through the rafters and set it off. Unfortunately whatever it was didn't trigger the lights, only the alarm sensor, so I couldn't just check it on my monitor, but the door was still firmly bolted and locked from the outside, so fingers crossed nothing has been snacking on our specimen.

Well today I should have been showing you the two best ways of emptying your acid bath. But there's been a change of plan. The trough should be full of a pinkish red sludge, instead there is little left except for the dried-up husk of whatever was coating the bath yesterday, and the minutest reside of what looks like a reddish meconium. For the security of the society and its trainees, I'm switching off the recording now, and will be removing the current link immediately. I will be back with you all as soon as I am sure that it is safe. But for now, adieu. I better go and deal with whomever or whatever has removed the remains of my specimen. Fingers crossed it was just a starving stray and not the police.

$\sim$

In response to your letter dated 27/05/2019
Monday 3rd June 2019, 09:52

The society apologises for the delay in responding to your complaint. We take our responsibilities to our members very seriously and will be issuing all trainees with a full refund for their course fees, and you will all be sent a complimentary e-code to attend any of our Lepidopterology starters courses for free, valid for the next 12 months only.

I know some of you have raised concerns over your original tutor, unfortunately he was not present when we visited his home address. Our team have of course ensured that no details of any trainees or members of the society were held at his address, and any incriminating evidence has been destroyed. There was no sign of a struggle or conflict at the address. The only odd thing noted by the investigators was the large number of chysalids that were hanging in his barn.

|Dendrochronology|

~

We're all storytellers here, though the staff have other names for us; delusional, fantasists, attention seekers, liars. We all have tales to tell, tales which are passed down through the halls, like the fairy tales of yore passed down through generations, from grandma, to mother, to child. Many of us don't have any family. There are those that never knew their parents, those whose relations are all dead and buried, or just those who are estranged; distance or embarrassment keeping them safely away. I see the looks of pity from the staff when visiting day comes around, but to be honest I'm quite glad that no one comes. Initially the hope and despair were painful, a pain that I had to get out of me somehow. But now I look at the newbies wearing their freshly laundered and ironed "outside" clothes. Sitting there, waiting. Shit-kicking grins plastered across their faces as they wait for their loved ones to come, but their smiles soon falter as their wives and husbands, fathers and mothers appear – their noses wrinkled at the smell of weeks of ingrained B.O., a greasy stench that worms its way down into the creases and crevices of the skin, and no amount of scrubbing with the harsh liquid soap on the wards can obscure. Their tentative kiss through a grimacing pout. Teeth clenched together, breath held to avoid the sweet rotting odour that results from one poor food choice too many in the canteen, and one too many nights of forgetting to brush your teeth before the night time meds trolley rattles round.

They say you can tell the age of a tree by the rings in its trunk, those lines equally portioning out the cycle of seasons. The tiny death as they sleep through the long, dark winter, and then the growth as they blindly reach upwards towards the bright, spring sun each year. If you look closely at us here I'm sure you could see our growth rings too, each one brought on by those little winters that we all have to suffer through. In a way though we are luckier than the tree; you don't have to cut us down to count our rings.

It was easy to miss it my first ring. I was so young, so small. A pliable sapling. I suppose in hindsight it was still visible if you knew where to look. It was there in my face. My mouth open in screams when the nightmares came, or in the fearful wide open circles of my eyes when he came instead.

The next ring was tiny. You wouldn't have known it was a ring unless you looked carefully. My mother asked me why I wasn't sleeping. Why I was waking her with my screams each night? That my father needed to get up early for work. That I didn't understand the hardship, what he did to look after us, what he had to put up with for us. That I was already tucked up in bed sleeping soundly, just like she was, by the time he came back from work, and he deserved his sleep. Even as young as I was then, I saw the injustice in it. It burnt so strong in me that I was worried that I'd burn up. That there'd be nothing left except for a pile of ash. So I told her. I told my mother what woke me at night. Not about the nightmares that made me scream, but about the ones that told me to be quiet, that placed a finger upon my lips as they turned me over and told me that my mother was asleep. I'd once tried telling him that I'd been asleep. I was tired too, couldn't he for once wake Mum, but he'd just smiled and told me if I was tired I could just close my eyes.

My mum had her own rings then, eyes wide in astonishment, mouth open even wider, as if she was going to swallow me. As she twisted the ring on her left hand. Round and round it went. I dropped my eyes and focused on it as it spun round; it was a bit tight, I could see the flesh either side bulging slightly where her fingers were swollen. Would she wear through it? Would she twist and twist, until it sliced straight through her finger? Would it be a clean break, would she wear it like a badge of honour? The rings perfectly formed of bone, and flesh, and skin. I concentrated on the sight of her ring turning, glinting in the evening light, while I waited. It stopped. The ring sat amongst her puffy flesh as I looked up at her face, the large ring of her mouth, now set into a much smaller one, lips pursed. She grabbed my shoulder and pulled me close. Her fingers digging in tight, she ground her thumb in the dip above my shoulder bone, she brought her face closer, her eyes dark circles, as she spat out the words "Dirty little liar."

The purple had started to bloom when I got out of my bath, the hot water drawing it to the surface. I'd run it too hot, my mum had refused to bathe me that night, so I'd drawn it myself, wanting to get myself clean, to scour away the words that my mum had spat in my face. But the water had been too hot, burning my foot as I stepped in, reddening my skin as I lay there, submerged. When I stepped out the ring was visible; a perfect, purple circle on my shoulder. I thought it would fade with time, I was wrong.

When I first arrived here, I told them the tale of my rings. I believed them when they said they wanted to help, their heads tilted bizarrely, their hands placed on the arms of the chair, fingers rigid against the swirling wooden grain, each tip resting against its own knothole on the varnished wood. I edged away, wishing that they wouldn't sit so close, cringing at the noise my chair made against the scuffed linoleum. Black marks streaked away from two circular indentations in the floor, and I was certain there'd be two more beneath me, signs of the endless weight of stories that this chair had endured. I looked up just in time as their hand reached for me. "It's okay. Don't worry. Those marks will clean right up. There'll be no sign of them tomorrow." I shrunk back into the chair as those questing fingers curled and retracted back into themselves, inches away from my creeping skin.

It was one of the old ones that explained it all to me. The doctors and nurses thought it would be a good idea to pair us all up, give the newbies a bit of peer support, and the old ones a sense of responsibility. Their names were marked next to ours in our admission files, and scrawled across the board secured to the wall next to the door – our only way in or out of the ward. Names marked with numbers and letters that meant nothing to me when I arrived: 17, 2, 15, ROW, WOOD.

All new patients are allocated an Old One. Mine was Jim Wood.

"Seventeen." Wood pointed at the number on the door. "This is where you'll sleep." The room was dark and sparse. Four beds stood divided from each other by four strange, small cupboards – each only big enough to hold a pair of shorts, t-shirt and a book. A grey papery-looking curtain cut the room in to quarters. "Though if yer know what's good for yer you'll only sleep in here. They..." he indicated out the door with his head "don't like yer staying in your room too long, says being on your own is the problem, yer need to be out there with the others to get better." He placed my bin bag of worldly possessions on the bed. "Oh and only sleep in here at night. They don't like it if yer sleep too much... *or* too little... I'll show yer later where we go if we wantta catch a nap without them spotting us."

The 2 was apparently my section. Wood smiled at that, told me it meant I didn't have to swallow any of their crap. "Literally" he told me. "Yer don't have to take the medicines, they can't make yer if yer don't wantta."

The 15 was for the minutes they would be checking on me. "At least yer not got a C for constant, can't even take a shit in peace then."

The ROW wasn't to do with boats at all, it stood for *Remain on ward*. "Don't worry, all the newbies are put on it, but if yer behave yer'll be allowed off, in a couple of days."

The doctor flipped through my file, before placing it on the desk. "So your father left?" He leaned forward in his chair, obviously his favourite interrogation position. He said I was difficult, that if I didn't talk to him, tell him what happened, he couldn't help me. But I knew that I couldn't have been the only difficult patient. His elbows rested on perfectly circular marks that they'd worn away on the chair's armrests, the wood pale under the eroded varnish. He may have sat like that for years, he must have done so for hundreds of patients. His fingers were carefully steepled, the whorl of each fingerprint snugly nestled against its opposing digit. The wood gradually yielding under the elbows of his suit jacket, like the centre of the stone steps that spiralled up into the clock tower in the hospital chapel.

I nodded.

"So how did he leave? Did your mother ask him to go after your... confession?"

I'm not sure why he insists on asking these questions; he has all of the answers in that thick file that sits on his desk. Everything about me is stripped raw and laid out upon those pages. He knows that my mum didn't kick my dad out. Though at least after I told her, he did stop coming to my room. Not, I think, because she believed me, but because he was worried that I might tell someone else who would. I'm not sure where he went; he left whilst I was at school and my mother was at her weekly hair appointment. When we returned there was almost no sign that he'd ever been there, his clothes, his shoes, the car all gone; the only evidence was the orange ring on the edge of the porcelain sink where his razor had sat. You'd think that I'd be glad that he'd gone, but the rings on my mother got smaller, her eyes narrowing as I sat down for tea, her mouth pursing tighter before she screamed that it was all my fault. The wedding ring that she never took off dug tighter into her fingers as they swelled from a mixture of cleaning fluid – from the job she now got up at five, six days a week for – and the vodka that she washed her nightly bottle of wine down with. Though swollen, they were still pretty deft, those fingers. Nimble in their movements as they pinched at my skin, red spots that looked like measles peppering my arms and legs. She was overworked, overwrought, overwhelmed. That's what they told me as I sat in the school nurse's office. She just had to go away for a while to rest, that I wasn't to worry about her. At that moment, though, I wasn't worried about her, I was worried about me. I'm not sure what kind of selfish monster that made me, but I didn't know how I was going to cope. I supposed I could make do eating cheese sarnies and crisps and drinking pop – that was all I could make myself, I don't think our oven even worked anymore – but I was scared about the nights, the dark. What if my dad came home? What if he came home and realised my mum wasn't there, that there was only me? What if they told him about Mum, and he was sent back to look after me? My face must have shown my fear, as the woman told me not to worry, that they'd found a house nearby for me to stop at. I wouldn't even have to change schools, and she'd take me round to meet my new family right away.

～

"You've got to understand that there's a synchronicity to it all." Wood was eating his roast beef, trying to saw through the tough meat with one of those blunt knives. They still didn't trust me with one of those, though I have no idea why. They can't cut butter, let alone anything else. So I was eating my roast dinner with a spoon, using a grubby fingernail to flick the cut up chunks of meat onto it.

"We don't get to choose who our newbies are, but we always find that they're right for us. The doctors'd say it's because they fink hard about our pairings, but that's bullshit. They don't know yer from Adam before yer arrive, so how could they?" Wood swirled his knife in a circle by his temple. "They all think we're mad, but look, it's circles. Once yer realise it all makes sense. We're looping. Everything has to go back to the start to finish, like that snake that ate its own tail. I'm Wood, and I'm here to the end, so it's only fitting that my tale is the start and end of it all. I'll tell yer it when you're ready "

I nodded. Wood was always prattling on about the tales. All of the old ones did. I'd only been in here a few weeks before I realised that they had to, that if they didn't they'd go mad, or madder. The old ones, weren't exactly the wise ones, they were the ones who were never getting better, never getting out. I'm pretty sure some of them hadn't even been ill when they first came; but whilst the door remained closed, the world outside grew until it was too big for them to find their way in it, and too scary for them to want to try. The realisation came about as my number 2 on the board was wiped cleared and instead of the "I" (for Informal) that I was hoping for, a number 3 was etched next to my name. Wood came to find me that day. He brought me a cake from the canteen, and placed it on the bedside table as I pretended to sleep, huddled deep in my fetid-smelling blankets.

"Get up. Yer know they don't like yer being in bed."

I didn't reply, there was no point. Doing what they wanted hadn't helped, it had just got me stuck in here longer. I heard the door close to, the light from the ward dimming as I reached out for the dry sweet cake he'd left beside me.

～

The next rings to appear were by my own hand. I hid them best I could from my foster family. They were nice, or at least my foster parents were; my sibling not so much. It was Adam that caused the rings, which was apt really as he was the ringleader. There are always those kids at school who you avoid. I think as a kid you instinctively know who they are and try to make yourself as invisible to them as possible. Well I was good at hiding. My Dad and Mum had taught me how to do that well. But I could no longer hide. Because Adam was *that* kid, and Adam was now my foster brother. Though I made sure never to call him that, he hated it. Hated that I lived in his house, hated that my being there somehow took something away from him. If he didn't get the latest sneakers it was my fault cos his parents had to buy two pairs of trainers now, so he only got shitty ones. I found a shit in my trainers on P.E. day when that was all kicking off. I blamed him, he blamed the dog. No matter what happened it was always my fault, and unlike the other kids he bullied at school, there was no escape once I got back home.

Those rings are larger. They twist and knot upon my skin, like the burn scars which warp the growth rings in the trees which survive forest fires. He may not have physically caused them – the hand that drew the compass point, the razor, the shattered glass, the rusted tin were not his – but it was his words, his threats of revelation, that guided my hand, that taught me to find a release, my fear gradually leaching away with the slow drawing of blood which marked my arms like tattoos. The first full ring occurred when he finally lived up to his promises. He'd wanted to go on a ski trip with the school, but his parents couldn't afford two tickets, and they said it wouldn't be fair for him to go and not me. I argued, I begged, I told them I didn't like skiing, that I hated the teacher that was taking the trip, that the kids going weren't my friends, I'd be happier at home. All true. But no matter what I said, it didn't help me plead my case with them, or with Adam. So he told. He told everyone, everything. About my mum, my dad, what they did, why I ruined his life.

They finally found me at my old house, the key snuck out from beneath the flowerpot at the back. I'd drawn a bath – as hot as was possible, from the old immersion tank – sat back and traced the rings, bracelets for me to wear upon my wrists. Unfortunately they found me, the bracelets becoming shackles as they dragged me away.

I thought back to that first admission. The hospital brighter than this one, modern. Posters of movie stars and photos of families and friends peppering the walls of the other patients' rooms, grease spots from aged blu tack marring mine. The other kids too skinny, too angry, too broken to be anywhere else. Hidden away, everything hidden. Hidden agendas, hidden tablets, food passed hidden under the table from those who wanted to starve their pain away to those who wanted to bury it under a layer of sweet gluttony.

I wonder how many of those children are here. Not *here* in this hospital, I've been in long enough that I'd know if they were patients here, but somewhere *like* here, another hospital, another prison, another street. Hidden away as we were all those years ago.

Wood sits with me daily. He watches as the food goes cold on my bedside table, he watches as the nurses check my gums and under my tongue for hidden tablets, he watches as they strip and wash my bed around me. The nurses don't mind him watching; it means that they don't have to. Whilst he watches he talks, about this and that, about who's moved on – to ICU or home, it doesn't matter – to who's kicked off, to what the staff are doing, tans and holidays, leaving days and cakes. In all those hours, in all those days, in all those weeks he doesn't tell me *his* tale, though.

When I finally leave my bed – threats of ICU and a great big fuck off injection in the arse spurred that decision – I asked him why he always spoke of the importance of the old ones' tales but had never told me his. He just shrugged and cut up my chicken for me.

My first hospital admission wasn't that bad, in all honestly. It was safe, most of the kids were okay, as were most of the staff. There's always going to be arseholes wherever you go, but there were far fewer in the hospital than there had been at school, so I could live with it. If I missed anything back then it was probably being outside. We rarely got to go out – not enough staff – so we all sat in front of the telly, getting pasty and eating the sweets that the nurses gave us – well, except for the anorexics who paced up and down the corridors like caged tigers, counting their steps alongside their calories.

I met my first girlfriend in there. I say my first, to date she's my only girlfriend. She told me we had to hide our relationship from the staff, that they frowned on that kind of thing inside, and that they'd split us up if they found out. I gave her my Procycladine; she gave me my next ring.

"We were lucky." she said.

When we were discharged we were sent to the same halfway house, both of us foster kids, both at that awkward age; too old for foster care, too young for adult services. Like many, we fell through the gaps, but we survived. A friend of hers rented us a flat, and our benefits and the bit of money she brought in on the side covered the essentials. "Don't ask," was always her answer if I ever enquired what she did to bring in the extra.

The next ring came when I found her rifling through my sock drawer. "What you looking for?"

She turned to me, her cigarette clamped between her teeth. "I need a smoke."

I pointed out that she had a smoke. It was a joke. She put it out on my arm, twisting as she replied, "Not now do I?"

After that it didn't seem to matter what I did. She stayed out later, said she was working – in her short skirts and cheap makeup – that someone had to make some money. But there always seemed to be less. Less money, less food, less heating as the gas was cut off, then the electricity. The only thing there was more of were the burns. She'd say I was making a fuss, that it was nothing, just a game, a bit of fun; she was surprised I could feel them at all under all that scar tissue.

I'd like to say I left her, but I didn't. She just disappeared one day. The only things left in her place were an eviction notice, a threatening letter from the landlord, and a mass of burnt puckered rings upon my skin.

∾

It's better here. I tell myself this every day when I wake dry and warm, and every night that I fall asleep safe and comfortable in my bed. I hear the others crying, keening for loved ones lost and locked out. The heavy doors they keep us behind, isolating us from those who are both our salvation and our destruction. But I don't cry, there's no one out there anymore for me, no mum, no dad, no partner or friend; the closest to love that I feel now I suppose would be to Wood, and that's more of an adoration on my part; a distant love, sparse and understanding on his own.

The nurses finished the work on my last ring yesterday, the stitches removed, the dressing discarded. Redness faded to a thin silver line around my now blind eye. You might think that I would hate the person who did this to me, who pissed on me as I slept in the doorway, then glassed me when I fought back, still half asleep, doped by alcohol and God knows what else. But as I study the carving, marvelling at the minute crosses stitched delicately upon my skin, gently pulling the two halves together, I'm glad. Glad that there's no more cold, no more hunger, no more fear. Glad that I no longer have to sleep on the streets, or in the filthy beds of the desperate souls who would pay for a night with me. Glad that finally I'm home.

"It's nearly time." Wood has been hinting that I'm nearly ready to hear his tale. His is the most important tale he tells me. "It's the tale of the door. Of the start and end of it all." He knocks his head with his fist, "Wood you see. The door's wood." He knocks his fist against his chest, "Wood in here, and wood out there." He laughs at his joke. I smile. I'm sure it must be funny, but the meds they've got me on have dulled everything; there's no lows anymore, but there's also no highs. I lost my laughter alongside my tears. Tears still glisten in Wood's eyes though as he tells me I'm ready. "You're an old one now…" he shifts closer, "…like me." He pulls me into an embrace as he whispers his tale in my ear.

They found him hanging the next day. The hospital is old, and although the wards are free of ligature points, the entrance hall is listed so they can't modernise it, and, well, there must have been at least one place remaining that was strong enough.

They had to cut him down to see his final ring. A band of blue and purple encircling his throat. Then they took him out the door that he'd held the tale of.

You want to hear that tale? I'm sorry but you're not ready for that. Maybe I'll tell you when you've been here a little longer.

|On the Island|

Halloween wasn't the same on the island as it was elsewhere. The children still made witches' hats and garlands out of construction paper, though the pumpkins were also cut out rather than carved; fresh vegetables being a scarcity on the rugged, windblown landscape. But the biggest difference was that Halloween on the island wasn't a time to honour the dead, but to bring forth the living.

The islanders had no wish to call back to those who had passed away, their bodies wrapped in tattered sails, their sacraments ballasted with sand and stone from the beach. Each pocket carefully weighed and filled, then sewn shut with fishing wire, before the body was taken far out to sea. Nobody wanted to remember their dead. Sentimentality had no place out here, and the candles that were lit on All Hallows Eve were not in hope to lure back those bloated, fish nibbled cadavers.

Sarah woke early that Halloween, the sky still dark as she made her way down to the shore, the bright, sharp, salt tang of the night's tide burning her nose, not yet overpowered by the stench of the seaweed; that would come later as it lay ripped and torn from the rocks, scattered across the sand for the wind and sun to bake. Sarah slipped off her shoes and placed them well out of the sea's reach before removing her clothes and folding them neatly one by one and placing them on top. Nestled within these layers she placed with reverence an earthen jar, her menses. She checked the wax seal. It would all be for nothing if her life blood seeped uselessly into the sand.

She was the first down this morning. Later the beach would begin to fill with others, girls that she known from school – though most of them younger than her. Brazenly stripping, teasing their friends who tried to hide their bodies beneath their hands before running quickly to the sea, allowing the chill water to hide their modesty. They may nod or smile at her, but fewer each year came to chat, as if with each passing year she became more of a pariah – alone, aging – as she came down to the shore once more. Sarah knew it was likely her last year to come down. Her parents regarded her with pity, the women of the island fear, the men disgust. She'd promised herself that if she wasn't successful this year then she would walk into the sea once more, but would not return. She didn't want their pity, and their fear was useless.

The sea water slipped over Sarah's ankles as she took her first tentative steps into the grey expanse. Cold as bone it gripped at her flesh, causing goosebumps to run up her legs. The first gentle tendrils of seaweed brushed against her skin like fingers, grasping, entreating her to stay, to sink down into the turgid depths. As she stepped further out the seaweed gave way to the delicate seagrass, the tendrils caressing her limbs. Each step deeper into the sea brought their gossamer touch closer to her divide, as the chill water slipped round her hips in its freezing embrace.

Each year she went further out, trying to find the best seaweed. The delicate seagrass for capillaries; for veins, knotted wrack; for arteries, oarweed. Praying that she would find the tangled masses unbroken this far out from shore. You could almost tell the ages of the women of the island by the depth that they ventured. The younger girls would spend the day frolicking in the shallows, jumping waves and splashing each other; more child than woman, they had no need of a mate, no matter what their body might say. The young women would venture further out, allowing the chill waters to bathe their bodies, each year venturing deeper and deeper, until there was only her. Submerged. Nothing showing except the gentle curve of her neck and her head, the waves matting her hair like the seaweed she coveted.

It was getting dark by the time Sarah ventured back out of the frigid waters. Her skin as wrinkled as the elders who sat mending the fishing nets in the hut down by the quay. She wended her way through the forms that lay like sunbathers upon the sand. Some haphazardly put together, left out for the gulls to pick at, or for the tide to take back; others carefully protected by the crags and outcroppings of the cliff walls. Although she had not seen them birthed, Sarah could tell which one, belonged to which girl. The elders of the island would tut or shake their heads at the carelessness of the young, but none of them would speak their disapproval out loud. If they wished for another year unfettered and barren than that was up to them.

Sarah carefully placed the weed down, the bladder wrack and gutweed, the sugar kelp and cock's comb. Layering each individual piece in their correct place. Once she was sure that everything was as it should be, she opened her jar, the thick liquid pooling at the centre of her creation. With one final glance she turned and made her way back up to village.

As her steps took her higher up the coast path, the sounds of revelry echoed down to her, the sweet sound of voices raised in song. The dissonance, as bawdy songs were belted out by innocent voices, brought to Sarah's mind the image of angels in a brothel. Sarah ignored the festivities and made her way back to her cottage. Those at the party wouldn't miss her, and she didn't want to remind them of what tomorrow might bring. Once home she settled in for the night, the fire lit, a blanket round her shoulders to fight off the sea chill that had worked its way down deep inside of her. She waited.

Sarah sipped at her cold tea. The night was quiet now, the festivities long past; the men asleep ready to get up at sunrise for a day's fishing; the women awake, excited and anxious as they strained to hear the sound of footsteps upon their path. The moon painted the island in shades of grey and silver as the first head appeared above the cliff edge, their hair, still wet and matted, glinted in the moonlight. Sarah watched the men appear as she waited to see if any of them would knock upon her door.

|Flowers|

~

Aptly, the first flowers arrived in spring. A sorry looking bunch, wrapped inexpertly in cellophane and tissue paper. Brown water stagnant in a blister twist at the base that only half of the stems actually reached to, the others cracked and dead, their flowers wilted, a shower of petals scattered across the pavement beneath the lamppost. It was a mystery as to why they were there, the card mottled and water stained, from either rain or tears, only said *In Our Prayers*; other than that the card was blank, neither saying who the flowers were for or from. There they sat propped against the lamppost in front of my house. I only saw them when I went to put the bins out, lying there forgotten, discarded, dead. Maybe they'd been tossed there in a pique of rage, an unwanted proclamation of love, stolen from the local cemetery. A thorn pierced my thumb as I picked up the bouquet, simultaneously lifting the lid on the bin, and throwing them inside without a second thought.

The second bouquet of flowers arrived the next day. These ones were equally as mangy, half of them dead, all of them past their best. Once they would have been cream, a pillow of fragrance, but now their petals were the colour of cerements, their smell sweetly pungent like incense. But these ones weren't just carelessly discarded: they were tied tightly to the post, a blue ribbon wound round and under and through the *No Parking* sign, plated and woven round the metal like a maypole. There was no card this time, no sign of why they were here, or who they were for. I made my way halfway down the road to grab my bin from where the dustman had deemed to leave it once they'd emptied it that morning. I checked each lamp post on the way, but there was no sign of flowers on any of the others. It was only when I got back that I noticed the bear, stuffed, holding a heart in its paws, a whimsical smiled stitched across its features. I picked it up; it was heavy, the fur sodden as if it had been sat out in the rain, but the pavement beneath was bone dry. Stale-smelling water dripped down my hands, drawing chill bracelets around my wrists. I debated putting the bear back, propping it upright against the lamppost, or even carefully balancing it on my garden gate so that whoever had lost it could come and rescue it. The bear looked as if it was well loved. But maybe it had just been dropped by the bin men, tumbled out of the bin lorry then blown along the road, until it ended up wedged against the streetlight. The brackish water continued to ooze from the bear, edging its way along my arms, soaking into the thin material of my shirt. My clemency towards the owner overcome by disgust, I lifted the lid of the bin and threw the sodden toy away.

I scrubbed myself raw in the shower; usually I'd have had a bath, but I could still feel the ice-cold track of that water on my arms, and the idea of lying in a bath, that liquid mingling with the warm water that enveloped me, made me nauseous. So instead I turned the temperature up on the shower as high as it would go and scrubbed myself with a flannel until my skin turned red.

Shivering, I dried myself in the steam-filled bathroom. Although the sun shone outside, I felt chilled to the bone. I hoped that I wasn't coming down with anything, that I hadn't caught anything from that foul bear. I bundled my clothes into the washing basket, and although it was still morning, I pulled my pyjamas out from where I'd neatly folded them beneath my pillow and put them back on. Grabbing my thick dressing gown from behind the bedroom door, I made my way back downstairs to search through the dust-covered tins in the back of the kitchen cabinets for something to eat.

It was while I was stirring a can of tomato soup on the hob – ignoring that it in fact went out of date the year before – that I heard the singing, a strange mix of reverence and raucousness that was only usually heard during midnight mass at Christmas once the pubs let out. The sound emanated from the front of the house. I turned off the hob and placed the lid over the saucepan to keep it warm, whilst I went to discover what the ruckus was about, the voices getting louder, raised as one as they sang. There was a dysphoria evident in the singers, their song growing the closer I got to the front door. A melody of sadness accented with ire. Passionate voices screaming the words of the hymn, as my hand turned the door handle. Then nothing, silence. I stepped out onto my front path, but the road was empty. I crept down the path, my stomach turning, sure that the singers must have hidden themselves behind the hedge that ran the perimeter of the garden. My heart thumped in time with my steps as I reached the end of the path, my hand shaking as I placed it upon the latch, but when I opened it, stepping out onto the pavement, it was empty. No one hiding behind the hedges, or running away up the street. Empty except for the wreath that lay propped against the lamppost.

The flowers kept coming; I stopped throwing them away after a couple of days, as it seemed to me that the more of them I threw away, the more of them were laid on the pavement. The lamppost was now a shrine, buried beneath the rotting blooms. After a week I contacted the council, sent them a letter complaining about the mess. Spring storms had blown in, severing the heads from the roses, and scattering the flowers down the road. Carnations and daffodils caught in my gateway, as cellophane flapped in the yew tree that shaded my patio, like a bird broken and torn, ripped from its nest too early.

There was no response from the council, no visit, no letter, no man with a broom sweeping up the detritus that littered the road in front. Instead, the flowers spread, new sprays placed on top of the snapped stems that tumbled into my garden each time I opened my gate.

I could have cleared the blooms away myself, stuffed them in the bin – it wasn't as if I ever filled it, living on my own. But it was the principle of the matter: I paid my council tax, it wasn't my rubbish, the council needed to come and remove it, it was what I paid them for. I kept an eye out for my neighbours; I didn't know any of them well enough to knock on their door, and complain about the mess on our street; but I knew them enough to nod and say hello to – when passing on our way to the shops, or when I got in my car to drive down to the social on a Friday night – but there was never anyone there when I looked out of the window, the inclement weather keeping them inside, no sound of mowers in the gardens, or of children playing football or riding their bikes in the street. So instead I tried to ignore the growing mound that blocked my path, and left the house by the side entrance, making my way down my driveway instead.

The stench was palpable, the cloying miasma of funeral homes and compost pits, the smell of decay heavy under the rotting sweetness, as if something had crawled under the blanket of rotting flowers to die along with them in a shroud of ripped plastic and wilting petals. The flowers lay the breadth of my garden now, garlands winding round the pickets of my fence, tendrils reaching along the borders that edged the garden. Dead heads lay rotting amongst the pansies and primroses that still bloomed bright, planted deep, grounded, their nutrients not sheared away in a florist. Although the day remained grey and overcast, the rain appeared to have blessedly stopped. I grabbed my gardening gloves from the shed and made my way to the edge of the garden.

Litter lay strewn across the flower beds: packets of sweets, their rainbow packaging faded and soft by the weather; cards and letters lay like papier-mâché on the cobbled path, each one leaving behind a ghost of itself as I peeled the shrivelled mess from the slabs. The mess on the street now flowed across the driveway; I'd have to move it, if I wanted to take the car out. It was disgraceful. I'd had enough. If the council weren't going to get off their arses and do something, then I'd have to do it myself. I slipped my hands into the gardening gloves, the elasticated cuffs rubbing and burning my wrists, the material stiff from not being used. Easing them off I made to tuck the sleeves of my jumper inside, red lines etched across my wrists. I checked the gloves for signs of thorns or nettles, for something that could have caused the irritation, but the gloves appeared clean, free of splinters or barbs But even through the thick wool of my jumper I could still feel the gloves cutting into my wrists as I picked up handfuls of flowers and stuffed them in the bin.

I collapsed, exhausted, on the sofa, burrs and leaves still stuck in the weave of my jumper, and switched the telly on. Flicking through the channels there was nothing to watch – an endless parade of movies that I'd hated when I'd originally seen them at the cinema all those years ago, or quiz shows with inane hosts and imbecilic contestants. I picked up the TV magazine and flipped through to find out what was on. It was only then that I realised that I had no idea what day it was. I thought back to when they'd last collected the bins, when I'd last been down for a drink and a game of snooker with the boys at the social. But the days all merged into one. I clicked onto BBC, checking the time on the carriage clock on the mantel and looking at the listing for Saturday, some kids' movie – *Cars* –, but there were no animated characters on the screen. I flicked to Sunday, but instead of my house filling with the sound of hymns, a chef was stood there cooking, smiling as they stirred the mixture in a bowl and spoke to the camera. Monday, Tuesday, Wednesday – the program wasn't advertised on any of the days in the magazine. I flipped to ITV, but it was the same, David Suchet twirled his moustache as Poirot, but there was no Agatha Christie scheduled to be shown. I clicked the button on the remote that the salesperson at the shop had told me would bring up the day's listings, but the screen died, glaring blue before the light dimmed and the screen went black. I pressed the on button on the remote to switch the telly back on but the light remained red. Even switching the power off and then on again did nothing to bring the telly back to life.

I headed into the hallway to phone someone, wording the question in my mind *Were we supposed to meet tonight?* So much better than *What day is it?* So much better than *Doctor, it's my memory.* I picked up the receiver, thankful that I'd written the infrequently-rung numbers down. I dialled the number for Tony down at the club, praying that his harpy of a wife didn't pick up the phone; for someone who ran a social club she was pretty preachy about the evils of alcohol, sighing at the customers as they ordered their pints, glaring at them as they headed off after closing to drive home. It wasn't as if we were drunk, just a couple of pints with the snooker; we weren't young lads out trying to drum up Dutch courage to ask out a lady, or middle-aged hustlers drinking away the stresses of the working week. There were no fights or vomit in the car park out back. If we could see straight enough to pot the black, then we were fine to drive home. The phone rang. I listened until it cut off, three beeps and a disembodied voice telling me to try later. I scanned through my address book, but there was no one else I could call, no one else that I was in touch with, the friends over the years dwindling away, taken away by ill health, or by their wives and families. I crossed each name out that I came to: Peter, cirrhosis; Steve, dead from a car crash; Andy, he hadn't been in contact since I feel asleep during the speeches at his second wedding. The only numbers left were Tony's or the doctors, and the idea of phoning there, of the questions my simple query would raise with the G.P., was too much to bear.

I checked my watch; the club would be in full swing by now, the lads that went there each day to escape from home racking up the balls. It was probably why Tony hadn't answered – he would either be busy pulling the pints, or if it was quiet, drinking one over a game. I could go and nonchalantly ask the date. They had a listing of the events by the door which said the day and date, I could check against it when I popped to the loo. No one would think it was odd if I couldn't remember the date, loads of people forgot that.

I carefully placed the address book back in the drawer and picked up my keys. Heading out I turned to face the garage, trying to ignore the mass of flowers that already blocked the gate.

Candles flickered on the fence posts at the end of the garden, the flames licking at the ribbons and plastic that draped themselves over the pickets. I headed over to blow them out. It was bad enough that people seemed to have decided that my house was some kind of roadside shrine or dumping ground. But I wasn't going to have my home go up in flames because of a carelessly left candle. Enough was enough; if the council wouldn't do anything, it would have to be the police. They could stake out the house, maybe check the CCTV that seemed to be everywhere in town. Surely they could fine whoever it was, slap an ASBO on them or something – this was vandalism, harassment.

Bending over I blew on the candle, but the flame didn't waver. Cursing my ancient lungs – years of smoking, finally taking their toll – I picked it up to snuff it between my fingers, but instead of wax, my fingers found plastic, the flame cold and hard between my fingers. Fake. I pinched the flame again, blew on it, turned it over in my hands, the switch on the bottom sheared away. Not knowing what else to do with it, I placed it back on the fence post, determined to call the police in the morning and have them haul everything away as evidence.

The flowers had edged their way down the driveway towards the garage. Kicking them out of the way I lifted the door and groped at the side for the light, my fingers finding it in the dark by instinct, and flipping it on. The garage flooded with light, but except for the work bench – dented where I drove my car into it one Christmas Eve – and an array of bent and rusty tools hanging on the walls, there was nothing there. A blank space, empty except for an oil stain on the floor to show where the car should have been. I stood dumbfounded: the door had been locked tight, and there was no sign of any break in. I couldn't believe anyone would want to steal my old rust bucket. It wasn't a good car, it wasn't a cool car; it hadn't even been a cool car when I bought it ten years before. The lads had laughed at it, called it an old woman's car when I pulled up at the club in it, but it was all I could afford once the insurance company wrote off the BMW, their rates shooting sky high for anything other than the small, sensible car that now got me from A to B.

I racked my brain, trying to figure out if I'd parked it somewhere else – maybe left it at the club after one too many – but I knew that I hadn't. Although it was old, the paint scratched and the body dinged, it had been instilled in me by my father not to leave things out, to put them away in their proper place. Even if my mind was wandering a bit further from home these days, I was sure I would have parked it back in the garage. I always did.

It wasn't an emergency as such, but I had no idea how else you could contact the police. I waited for the operator to answer, for the rebuttal about calling 999, rather than waiting till morning and going to the station. The phone rang; I counted the rings, trying to calm the anxiety in my chest, that fear that I'd done something wrong, although I knew that I hadn't. *One, two, three,* it's okay, I'm the victim here, *four, five,*

six, they'll understand, they wouldn't expect an old man to walk all the way to town to report a crime, *seven, eight, nine*, the fear in my stomach twisted in indignation, good job I wasn't being threatened at knife point by a burglar, *ten, eleven, twelve*, the ringing stopped, cut off, dead. "Hello" I spoke, knowing that the silence wasn't just a moment's pause, a gathering of the operator's thoughts. "Hello." I pressed the hook switch, but the silence continued. I hung up the phone, then lifted it back to my ear, but the only sound was the whoosh of air. It reminded me of the conch shell that I'd found on the beach as a kid, of cradling it against my ear at night, the sound twisting and echoing the waves that I'd played in during the day, lulling me to sleep.

Panic twisted, shooting through my gut, my anxiety and fear elevating, as I wondered if someone had cut the wire. Maybe the same person who stole my car. I had nothing worth stealing, but they could take it all. I looked towards the front door, aware that I hadn't locked it when I'd come in to call the police. The door loomed black against the darkening night. Twilight lay heavy, but the streetlights remained off. Opening the door I scanned the street. I knew none of the neighbours; those that had been here when I moved in, now dead or moved on; those that replaced them generations younger, the divide too wide to bridge. Family homes filled with families. The houses all stood dark, no lights on in kitchens, not even the flicker of a telly. Was I safer in here or out there? What if the person who stole my car was out there waiting for me? But what if they'd already snuck in earlier when I was watching the telly, or having a shower?

I scanned the street once more, looking for any sign of light, of life. Panic wreathed its way around me, indecision planting my feet firmly on the threshold. At the same time terror detached me, I felt like an observer, distinct, apart, an actor in a movie. I stood in the centre of a maelstrom, a void, nothing, and at the same time integral to the vortex that threatened to drag me down.

I reached out to switch on the hallway light, hoping that someone would see my distress call in the dark. That the situation would be lessened in the light. The hall remained dark. I tried the porch light but there was nothing. A wave of understanding and calmness drowned out the panic that had been growing inside me – a power cut, nothing more sinister than that. It would explain the dead line, and the black and empty street. I shut the door, locking it and for once throwing the chain across too. I couldn't cook anything for dinner, but there was a bottle of whisky in the larder that would help settle my stomach enough to sleep.

The morning sun streamed through the window. Everything looked better in the stark light of day, no monsters lurking under the bed, though the lights still didn't work, and the phone remained silent when I picked it up. I hated the bus, but I had to do something; I couldn't just wait around for the power company to fix the electric, it could take days. I couldn't wait that long to phone the police. I didn't have a car. I had to report it, get a crime number or an incident number, or whatever it was the insurance company needed. That car was my lifeline, without it I couldn't get to the club, the buses didn't run that late round here, and I couldn't afford taxis, not on the pittance of a pension that I bought home each week.

The flowers tumbled onto the door mat as I opened the front door, the path beyond strewn with bouquets and posies, like the aisle of a church on a bride's wedding day. I moved through them, the petals crushed, the leaves crumbling beneath my foot. The withered blooms disintegrating beneath my feet, crackling like the leaves in autumn that hide the winter's rot away beneath them. Each step punctuated, a crunching like the sound of small bones, of a chicken wing cracking between my teeth, grease coating my hands, of roadkill and raptors feeding on carrion broken beneath tires. The memory of the neighbour's cat, the sound of my tyre going over its small body, the dull plonk, then the silence only broken by my whispered entreaties. *Please be the cat, please be the cat.* My footsteps stumbling as I stepped from the car, whisky and fear burning my stomach as I reached down, blood on my hands as I lifted the broken body up. The weight heavy in my arms, for something so small.

|Behind a Broken Smile|

~

"It's only for a couple of weeks. You used to love going to your nan's."

I huddle down into my coat, the zipper pulled high, trapped between my teeth as I chew on the tab, slipping it over my snaggletooth, tasting the metal with my tongue.

"It might be the last time you get to see her. She's not getting any younger, and… it's been a long time."

I want to ask her whose fault she thinks it is that it's been a long time. Whether, if Dad was still alive, she would have thought it was so important I stayed at my nan's, instead of at a friend's house. In my pocket my phone vibrates against my fingertips, wanting to know where I am. Why I'm late. I pull it out and tap out a quick message; I don't respond to my mum.

"Where are you going?"

"Out." I pull open the door.

"When will you be back?"

I close the door behind me and walk up the path.

~

"Sounds like a right bitch."

I'm not sure if he means my mum, or me going away. He's got his arm round me, pulling me into him away from the cold. He doesn't like my coat; I can tell by the way that he looks at Kelly, lounging on the other bench with her boyfriend. His arm rests under her vest top; her arms pimpled with goosebumps. I snuggle back down into my coat, the zipper wedged firmly in my mouth. His hand strokes my face and tries to ease it away; it pulls against my tooth as he murmurs, "How am I supposed to kiss you with that there?" I tighten my lips around the tab, before realising that I'm unable to answer. Instead, I slide along the bench, stamping my feet to warm them. I tuck my hands into my sleeves before standing.

"I've got to get back now, Kelly." I can only see the back of her head, as her boyfriend stares at me across her shoulder. Her only response a flip of the hand as she continues to kiss him. I leave quickly before anyone can offer to walk me home, but no-one does.

"Now it's been a long time, you've got to remember that your nan isn't as young as she used to be."

I'm not sure if I want to shout at my mum that it's her fault; or whether I want to point out the stupidity of her statement.

Mum reaches out to knock, her hand trembling as the tentative tap dies on the door. "Don't mention your dad."

I remove my hand from my pocket and rap firmly against the wood. "What if Nan mentions him first?"

Before Mum can formulate an answer, the door opens. I look down. My nan stands in front of me, tears in her eyes.

"Come in."

She's so small. She always seemed to tower over me, but now she's shrunk, withdrawn into her skin, frail and fragile. Everything about her is tiny, as if her life, her essence, her whole being has been drained from her body.

"Come in."

I step inside; Mum falters on the step. I don't offer her any support, if anyone deserves to feel awkward here, it's her. I can taste copper. The zipper tab has worked its way into my mouth again. My mouth warms the cold metal as I hook it back over my tooth.

"I'll take you up to see your room, shall I?"

Nan closes the door behind my mum's retreating back – she hadn't stayed long, pleading an early start the next day. But I saw the way her eyes flickered round the living room and the photos that adorned the walls and sideboard: images of her wedding day, of Dad, of me, but only as a little kid.

"I've put you back in your old room. I'll sort us out some tea while you unpack."

I look around the room, listening to the heavy footsteps of my nan as she makes her way downstairs. How so much noise could come from such a small person is beyond me. My friend's families always joked about how quiet I was when I was little. How their kids sounded like baby elephants parading round their bedrooms as if marching round a Big Top. I always stayed quiet, silent, my step light, my body insubstantial, a ghost hidden within my home, my room, my clothes.

The room hasn't changed much since I was last here. The rainbow striped flannel sheet and lilac blanket may have been the ones I slept under as a kid. The double bed looms in the tiny spare room, no more than a foot each side to squeeze round. I was petrified of that bed when I was little, sure that the blossoming softness of the mattress would swallow me whole when I crept into it at night. The enormity of it against my single, child's bed at home.

I complained to my nan about it after my first overnight stay, told her excuses, rather than the truth. Told her that the bed was too high, that I couldn't get off. That the bed was too large, that there was nowhere left for me to play. Told her everything and nothing. Anything to swap that bed for my children's one at home. But she just smiled, weary at my entreaties, and told me to hush, that there was nothing that could be done; her house was small, her family more important than childhood games. There was only one spare room, and Nan said she had to have a double, two singles wouldn't fit, and she had to have space so we could both stay over when we came to visit. It was a twist to the platitudes my father told my mother as to why she couldn't stay. Placating her with the temptation of nights out with friends instead of just another boring evening in front of the telly. It wasn't as if it was going to be fun visiting his mum: a duty, nothing more. That there wasn't room for all three of us to squeeze into the tiny spare bedroom. She should be glad that she didn't have to go, most wives would jump at a ready-made excuse to avoid a night at their mother-in-law's. That she should go out and enjoy herself, like she did when they first met. Do her hair and her makeup, put on some pretty clothes and go and have fun, like she did before me.

My mother didn't notice my silence after that first visit. My father carrying me upstairs as I burrowed my face into the hood of my parka, instead of the curve of his shoulder as I used to. My body stiff under his arms, rather than clinging to him as someone safe; my protector, my father.

He whispered to me as he undressed me for bed, my hands fluttering like doves that he knocked away as I tried to cover my body until he pulled the nightgown over my head, tapping me on the bottom as he jovially announced that it was time for me to climb into bed.

There was no change to his routine when we got home. No acknowledgement of the previous night, no apology for the burning pain that caused me to weep when I urinated. Just a whisper that he loved me, another telling me that I shouldn't speak, that I should just go to sleep like a good girl. It was late, and Mother was tired, and I didn't want to upset her now, did I? Saying that he was sure I knew how to be a good girl and go straight to sleep.

He stood in the door as my mother said goodnight. Framed in the doorway watching as she swept my fringe away from my face to plant a kiss on my forehead. A perfect tableau. I felt tears prickling at the back of my eyes. For a moment my mother's face changed, her eyes darkened, the laughter lines cutting deeper in worry. My father still stood behind, watching over us.

Unable to stem the flow of tears for much longer, I closed my eyes and rolled over, away from my mother's hand and watchful eye. By the time she switched off the light my pillow was already wet.

The night-time visits from my father coincided only with the trips to my nan's. I'm never sure how or what my mother found out. In the same way that I didn't speak to her that first night, she didn't speak to me on the last. There was no scene, no shouting, or screaming, no items hurled or smashed, no voices raised in anger. Just a request that I eat my tea in my bedroom, to use the bathroom now, and not to come out again until she came to fetch me.

There was a bowl of chicken nuggets on my bedside table – my favourite. It was what I always ordered when we went out, whether to McDonalds or to a fancy restaurant. A bar of chocolate lay on my pillow, like I'd heard they did at posh hotels. She'd even brought the telly upstairs – one of those heavy, hulking old-fashioned cathode-ray tube ones, not the flat screen ones of today. It must have given her a hernia lugging it up all those stairs. I switched it on, the image was fuzzy, the sound almost non-existent. I flicked through the channels, but without being able to plug it into the aerial it was unwatchable.

I heard a car pull up, the sound of gravel under tires, and the crunch of my father's footsteps on the drive, his cheery hello and the slam of the front door as he closed it behind him. Then silence, before the low murmur of my mother's voice as she spoke, her words nothing, masked behind the white noise of the television. I crawled out of bed and crept to the window, pinching the curtains between my fingers as I peeked out. My father stepped back out onto the front path, a suitcase in each hand. I presumed Mother had packed them, hidden them away from me in the lounge so I wouldn't freak out when I saw them, panic that we'd be going away, that *I'd* be going away.

My father looked up at my window, his mouth opened to speak; I'm not sure if he saw me hidden away behind the nets, peeking out between the chink in the curtains, but he closed his mouth again without uttering a word, my silence now his as he slunk away.

I hadn't seen my nan since that day. She sent Christmas cards and Easter eggs, birthday presents, and money on the day of my confirmation. These parcels arrived with two sets of gifts within, one from her, and one from my father. My mother always allowed me to keep the presents from my nan, but unceremoniously sent my father's ones back *Return to Sender*. No note, no thank you card, just the parcel sealed back up and a line through our address. She didn't even bother to write my nan's address on the package. I don't know if those parcels ever got returned, or if instead they sat in some huge warehouse somewhere, the toys unplayed with, the books unread, the chocolates rotting and melting deep inside, until some rat gnawed through the cardboard and faded wrapping paper to get to the spoiled goodness within.

I wished my mother had returned them properly, so that he knew we didn't have them, knew we didn't want them. That maybe it would stop him sending me the trinkets and toys that I would never have been able to bring myself to touch. That he would stop sending me selection boxes and Easter eggs that I could never stomach to eat, knowing that his hands had picked them out and oh so carefully wrapped them.

I wanted to ask my mum to go there and scream at him to stop. That I had nightmares that he was watching me playing with the toys that he sent, that he dreamt of me opening his gifts with joy on my face. I didn't even want to be in his thoughts, in his memories. But I never did ask my mother. I watched her cross out our address and write *Return to sender* in her neat no nonsense handwriting, and never once did I ask. Not wanting to answer the questions from her that my request might elicit.

"Tea's up." My nan's voice comes echoing up the stairs. My bags remain where I left them, zipped and locked by the bedroom door. I don't want to unpack, to place my things where his had been, to hang my clothes on hangers that used to hold his. I can't even bear the thought of my skin touching the sheets where he'd lain.

I run to the toilet and vomit, ignoring the repeated calls to tea from down below. *It's only for two weeks.* I parrot my mum's words. I'm safe here, there's nothing to fear, it's just me and my nan. A chance to bond again after all those years. It's not as if my dad is going to pop round for tea, that I'll go downstairs and find him sat at his old chair at the scratched Formica table in the kitchen. He's down the road, buried under six foot of earth.

I hadn't gone to the funeral. Nan contacted us to tell us about it; the envelope adorned with her beautiful copperplate handwriting, the letter folded neatly, several pages long, to tell us that her son had passed away. So many words when all she needed to put was the date, time and address. So many words that my mother read, dry-eyed, before ceremoniously burning the invitation on the barbeque out back.

The day after the funeral another letter arrived, the envelope thin, containing nothing but the order of service. There had been no more letters, no more parcels, no card upon my birthday or at Christmas. Nothing until my mother broke her silence and wrote pleading for clemency, for Nan to look after me while Mum was away with work. A one-off she promised me; the first of many, a new start, she promised my nan. I knew she was lying; I just didn't know who to.

I sit pushing the lumps of meat round in their congealing jelly, my face sweating in the stuffy kitchen, stomach turning as it had done each time I had sat here before.

"Never mind, love. It can do that to you, travel. Maybe some toast later if your stomach settles enough."

Nan methodically cuts her faggots into bite-size pieces, each one the same size as the mouthful before. I don't mention that a half-hour car ride was hardly what I'd call travel.

"Oh, that reminds me. I've got something for you." She swallows her last piece of faggot, places her knife and fork neatly together on the plate, and takes a sip of tea. "Something to help you sleep a bit better, you know, with you being in a strange bed and all that. Sometimes a change of scenery can be disconcerting to the young, make them imagine things that aren't there, give them nightmares." She pulls out the seat at the head of the table.

For a minute I think I'm going to be sick again, vomiting straight onto the plate of food in front of me, as I expected my father's face to pop up from underneath the table, hiding away beneath the seat that he always sat on, ready to grab at my dinner and exclaim *Faggots, my favourite.* For him to reach over and pinch at the fat that bloomed on my hips, at my thighs, at my breast and announce *Well, if you're not I will, waste not want not, and all that.* But instead, what my nan produces from beneath the table is a doll – a rag doll, floppy and boneless, the material worn and faded as if well loved.

"I made it for you." She passes it over to me.

It's an odd doll, no Raggedy Ann or Andy. Instead of the usual dress or romper suit or other childhood attire, this doll wears a three-piece-suit, each piece exact, even down to the tie and the tiny cuff links that hold the shirt sleeves in place. It would look quite dapper if it wasn't for the face: leather, stretched and stitched, the nose non-existent under the tension of the material. The button eyes – although creepy – aren't too odd; it's the smile, not sewn on in bright red thread or felt, but a zip that runs the width of the doll's face. Instinctively I reach for my neck, for the zip on my coat to hook over my tooth, but remember that it's hanging in the closet, my nan having insisted that I put it away, that it looked like I wasn't staying if I wore it in the house. The zip on the doll's face is nothing like the one on my coat; whereas that one had been worn away, corners smoothed, moulded to the bite of my jaw, this one is bulky on the face of the doll, the teeth brown with rust, flakes of it gathering at the pull, like the doll had a cold sore at the corner of its mouth.

"Well, do you like it?"

My fingers tug at the zipper, but it's rusted shut, stuck in a manic grin.

"It took me ages, wore my fingers to the bone making it for you. I started it as soon as your mother told me you were coming to stay. I hope you're not too old for dolls. It's just for show really, I don't expect you to play with it. I thought you could put it on your bed, you know, make the place homely. I know how much that bed used to frighten you when you were little, the tears at bedtime as if it was a monster that would swallow you whole."

How much does she know? How much has my mother told her? How much does she suspect? Does she know that the monster wasn't the bed, it was *in* the bed?

"Why don't you go up and pop it in now? Then I'll make us some hot milk to settle your stomach before bed. You were always a delicate little thing, always complaining of this or that. I suppose it was to be expected the first time, staying in a strange house, but you were fine that first night, all smiles and goodnight hugs and kisses. It wasn't until the next trip that you got all worked up over that bed until it made you sick."

I smile, glad of her inane nattering; there's no expectation of an answer to her questions, which was good as there is none that I could give. I head upstairs, holding the doll carefully by the sleeve, not wanting to touch the clammy leather of its flesh. I open the door and scan the cramped bedroom; there's no way I'm going to put the doll in the bed. The touch of the sheets will be bad enough, but the accidental touch of the doll in the night would, I'm sure, send me into paroxysms of terror, my half-asleep brain weaving its touch into my nightmares until I couldn't tell dream from reality, doll from the touch of a hand.

All I really want to do with the doll is to shove it in the back of the wardrobe until I leave, burying it there to rot, pretending dismay that I'd forgotten it when I left. But that might mean my nan would post it on to me. Maybe I should leave it tucked in the bed on the last day, tell my nan that I want it to stay here until the next time I stay. But then she might expect there to be a next time, and that's not going to happen. I'm not sure what kind of emotional reunion my mum thought this visit was going to start, but it's been too long. Nan and her house are so intrinsically linked to my dad that my fear and revulsion for one are indistinguishable from the other.

I shove the doll onto the bedside table, propping it against the wall, so its boneless body sits upright. It flops down, its face looking at me once more. I twist it away slightly, so it's staring at the wardrobe rather than the bed. I still know it's there, but I sleep on my side, I can turn my back on it, pretend it doesn't exist. It may be creepy, but it's harmless, a doll. An ugly one, but just a doll.

It's still light out when I make my excuses and head up to bed, pleading exhaustion after the long day. I check my phone but there are no missed calls from my mum, just a curt text message saying *Sorry really busy, will call you tomorrow. Night x.* My finger hovers as I debate whether to reply or just to delete it; instead I lift the phone. "Say Cheese." I take a photo of the doll and upload it to Facebook. Wait for the comments to flood in about the creepy-ass doll. Scrolling through my feed, I see photos of my friends, of Kelly and her boyfriend, of Kelly with *my* boyfriend. I'm disgusted at the images of her lying sprawled in his lap, of his hand in her hair, of the smirks on their faces as they pouted to the camera. I don't care about him; he was my boyfriend in name only, because a boyfriend was what was expected. It was what he wanted, what Kelly wanted, or so I thought. I couldn't care less about him, but the betrayal from my supposed best friend still hurts; and the fact that she spread it out across Facebook makes it worse. Their gurning faces, sly in the knowledge that I'd see, that I'd know. I switch my phone to silent and plug it in to charge.

The doll has moved. My stomach jumps into my throat, bile mixing with the minty taste from my toothpaste. I lift my wash bag to my mouth and chew at the zip, the shiny pull snagging and sticking on my tooth. The doll has slid down the wall, its body face down on the side, as if it's trying to crawl its way into the bed. I concentrate on the taste of metal in my mouth; I must have knocked the bedside table when I plugged the phone in. I pick up the doll and wedge it against the wall, the material slippery beneath my fingers, as if the doll had been dipped in grease, leaving a patina of residue on my hand. I wipe my fingers on my trousers, unwilling to leave the room again to wash them, worried that if I do I'll come back and find that the doll has moved once more. That I'll find it on the bed, or *in* the bed. Lying there between the sheets, that rusted smile bisecting its head. I climb into bed fully clothed. The touch of the pillow on the naked skin of my cheek feels like spiders crawling on my skin. I think about putting my coat on, pulling the hood up, tucking my hands within its voluminous sleeves and hooking the zip over my tooth. But I can just imagine the telling off I'd receive if my nan came in to check on me. So instead, I lie back on my pillow, my hair cushioning my head from its touch, no longer wanting to turn my back on the doll.

I bite back the scream as the nightmare wakes me, not wanting to bring my nan running. I reach over for the bedside lamp, knocking my phone onto the floor as my hand sweeps the unfamiliar side to find the switch. Light floods the room, the ceiling so familiar, although it's been so long since I last saw it. The cracks and pitting are a constellation that as a child I wished I could be whisked away to. It's fine, I'm safe, there's no one here. I'm in bed, on my own. My breathing calms as I realise the only things touching my skin are my clothes; the only things digging in are the rumples and creases of material, nothing warm, nothing hard, nothing human.

I close my eyes and count, allowing my heartbeat to slow. Thinking about the weight of the blankets on my body, willing myself to calm. Telling myself I'm safe. That for once, here at my nan's, I'm safe. That I can close my eyes, here in this bed, alone. I open my eyes and roll over to grab my phone off the floor. The scream grows again in my throat as I see the doll sat slumped on the floor, its rump squarely on my phone. It seems to leer from its half-open zip mouth as it stares at me. I pull the blankets closer round my neck, trying to shroud my body from the glazed glare of its button eyes. Revulsion courses through my veins, nerves tightening, as my body tries simultaneously to flee and shrink itself into the corner, making itself as small a target as possible. A child once more, hiding away in the shadows, hoping that I won't been seen, that I'll be overlooked just this once. I try to persuade myself that I'd knocked the doll off when my phone fell, that I'd heard two thumps, not one, in the dark.

Light has started to etch itself around the curtains by the time I manage to extricate myself from within my blanket cocoon. *It's just a doll,* I tell myself as I reach towards it. *Nothing more than an old woman's attempt to reconnect with her granddaughter.* A wildly inappropriate gift for a fifteen-year-old, but to her I'm probably still that six-year-old little girl, who cried for her mummy at night and hugged her doll so tight that it looked like its head was going to pop off.

I twist the key in the wardrobe door, stuffing the doll amongst the suits and boxes within; a waft of my father's aftershave creeps out, permeating the room and masking the scent of damp and air freshener that hangs in the air. Despite the cold dawn, I open the window to the sound of birds heralding the day.

The day passes slowly. I check my phone, hoping to at least have some kind of contact with my mates, but my feed is full of images of Kelly and Steve, my boyfriend – my ex-boyfriend I suppose. Photos of her pouting for the camera, his hand on her thigh, or under her top. The sight triggers something in me: not anger, not upset; fear… but not for me. I mute Kelly's posts; it feels like a betrayal, worse somehow than the one she committed against me. I don't care about Steve, although she's not to know that, but I still care for her. I just can't bear to see, to watch them, to watch her.

Without Kelly, my social media soon fills up with vacuous memes and mindless videos of people I don't know, doing stuff I couldn't care less about. A mindless balm that soothes my nerves. After lunch I manage to excuse myself, blaming my period and telling Nan I'm going for a lie down for a while.

"You've grown so much, a proper little lady now." Nan slowly stands, one hand pressing against the arm of the chair to lever herself up. "You'll be settling down with kids of your own some day. You go on up, love. I'll get you a hot water bottle."

It's sat between the two pillows when I open the door. Its head back, limbs sprawled suggestively across the tightly tucked in sheets and blankets. I'm still standing in the doorway staring at it, trying to build up the courage to touch its slippery body, when I hear my nan's cumbersome footsteps make their way up the staircase.

"Come on then, love, let's turn this bed down and get it warmed up. Nothing worse than a cold bed is there, especially when you're on your own." She winks at me. "No one to warm your feet on. Here, hold this."

She presses the doll into my hands before deftly flicking the sheets back and burying the hot water bottle at the foot of the bed.

"That'll warm up nicely for you now."

She turns, arching her back, the pops loud, audible even to me as she stretches.

"It'll last a long time that doll, not like those cheap things that you can buy at the store. Hand-stitched. The secret is to make them out of the material you'd make your own clothes from. Hardy it is, won't wear, no matter how many times it gets cuddled, or left outside, or dragged through the mud. Yes, that mud will wash straight off, you can just stick it in the washing machine and it'll all be as good as new. That doll will still be pristine when your own children play with it. Now, you go on and have a good rest. I'll call you when it's dinner time."

The door closes; I wait until I hear her footsteps receding down the stairs and the sound of the kettle whistling on the stove. The high-pitched noise is an accompaniment to the radio that plays incessantly in the kitchen throughout the day, no matter what else she might be doing.

I tip-toe over to the wardrobe. Holding my breath, I open the door and stuff the doll deep in the back behind the old shoe boxes and board games that are stacked beneath the hanging clothes. I lock the wardrobe door and don't breathe again until I open the window, the curtains billowing in the breeze. Making my way to the bed, I flip the pillows over, careful not to touch where the doll had been sat, and lie down fully clothed. But even with the pillows turned and the windows opened wide, the smell of my father's aftershave still lingers on the bedclothes.

"Dinner!"

The sound echoes through the darkness. I wonder why on earth someone would want dinner in the middle of the night, before I realise that I have my eyes shut. The blackness isn't absolute; there's a redness that tinges the edges. I open my eyes, groggy, my limbs heavy, my neck stiff where the draught from the window has caught it. I hadn't even realised that I'd been asleep. Exhaustion and a couple of nights of broken sleep with the anxiety about this visit had overcome me, knocked me for six.

I twist, swinging my legs round to sit on the edge of the bed; my foot catches something and sends it spinning across the room.

"Shit," I mutter under my breath, sure that I'd fallen asleep with my phone again. It'd be just my luck if I broke it whilst I was here. But the phone is on my bedside table. There, in the corner of the room, lies the doll, crumpled, its head between its legs, as if trying to do a handstand against the wall. "Shit."

I make my way over, intending to pick it up and lock it in the wardrobe again. Nan must have snuck in and placed it on the bed with me whilst I slept. I don't want to hurt my nan's feelings, but maybe if I lock it in the wardrobe and hide the key, she won't realise. I expect she must have come in to put something away and seen it there, though I'm surprised at how heavily I must have slept for me not to have heard her and woken.

I pick up the doll, and turn the wardrobe's handle, but the door doesn't shift. I pull again, but the door isn't stuck – it's locked, and the key is no longer there.

I bring the doll down and sit it in the chair at the head of the table, then wash my hands before sitting down to eat. I dislike the idea of the doll sitting there watching me, but I hate the idea of it being in my bedroom whilst I'm not there to see it. I'm sure that if I had left it discarded in the corner, or hidden in a drawer or beneath the bed, I would go upstairs after dinner and see it leering at me from the bed once more, even if no one else had been up there to move it. So I brought it down, and wedged it on its seat, on *his* seat.

"I'm glad you like it, love." Nan places a plate of grey meat and overcooked veg in front of me; the gravy, weak and greasy, shines on the plate. "I wasn't sure if you liked it, whether you thought you were too grown up now for dolls and the suchlike."

I shook my head, taking a mouthful of chalky boiled potatoes to excuse my lack of response. While I eat, I consider what to do with the bloody thing. Can I sneak a question about when the bin men come into the conversation without garnering too much suspicion? I don't want to just chuck it in the bin; Nan might see it in there, and I don't want to hurt her feelings. But the idea of sleeping with it in the same room as me for another night, let alone another two weeks, is unbearable. Even looking at it makes my skin crawl. Although it only has buttons for eyes and a zip for a mouth, it seems sentient. Human isn't the right word for those dead blank stitched on buttons, or the mouthful of cold metal teeth. But then there are people I've met who'd have that same cold, dead look about them when they smile, when they leer. Predatory like a shark, each tooth ready to pierce flesh.

"I might pop out after tea, Nan." I take another mouthful of chalky potato. "Just up to the shops. Is there anything you want me to pick up?"

"I don't know if that's a good idea, love. It's getting late."

"It's only just gone six…"

"I don't think he'd like it."

"You don't think who'd like it?"

"Oh… Your mum. I mean, I don't think your mum would like it."

"She'd be fine with it. I'm allowed out till nine during the holidays, and it won't be dark for ages. I'm only popping up the road to the shops anyway."

Nan stares across the table, lost in thought, her eyes focused on the doll that sits across from her.

"I only want to get some stamps, you know, to send letters to my friends. I miss them." I have no intention of sending a letter to anyone; to be honest, I'm not even sure how to go about it. It's not as if we tell each other our postcodes when we arrange to meet up.

There's a moment when I wonder if I'll have to repeat myself, as my nan just sits there blankly staring across the table. I want to stand up and check if she's blinking. To wave a hand in front of her eyes and see if her pupils follow the movement. To raise a fist and thrust it towards her face just to see if she'll flinch, just to check that I'm not now sitting having dinner and conversation with a creepy-ass doll *and* a corpse. But before I can slide my chair back, she smiles, a grin cutting her from ear to ear. So reminiscent of the doll's zippered mouth, set there in her leathery skin, that for a moment it seems as if she could have birthed the doll rather than sewing it together with fabric and thread.

"Oh, you don't have to put yourself out dear. I have some stamps in my handbag. I'll go get them after dinner. Do you have space for dessert? It's peaches and condensed milk."

I take the doll with me into the bathroom when I go to brush my teeth, stuffing it in the airing cupboard. I didn't want it watching me get undressed, those predatory eyes shining as I slipped my pyjamas on, but there was no way that I was going to leave it in the bedroom unattended. I might have returned to find it sitting on the bed, tucked in deep between the blankets, or propped up against the headboard. Worse would be if I went back in and couldn't find it at all; I wouldn't be able to sleep until I found it. I'm pretty sure that if it went missing within my room, I wouldn't sleep for my entire stay, and that by the time Mum came back to pick me up, I'd be a gibbering wreck, raving on about dead eyes and shark's teeth that glinted in the darkness ready to eat me up, like the wolf hiding in grandma's bed in *Little Red Riding Hood*. Hysterical tales of dolls and night terrors, of the scent of aftershave, and of things that were both present and absent.

To be fair, I already feel as if I'm halfway to the loony bin as it is, hiding away from a doll. Like a child whose toys change to monsters under the shadows of the night.

I pull the doll back out from between the towels and flannels and make my way back into my room, calling *night* to my nan as I go.

"I'll be straight up with a cup of hot chocolate for you, love."

"It's okay, Nan, I've already brushed my teeth."

"It's already on the hob. I just won't add any sugar. You get yourself in to bed and I'll be up in a jiffy."

The wardrobe's still locked, the key absent from the door. I empty the top drawer of the dresser, stuffing my pants and socks in with my t-shirts in the second drawer down, before hiding the doll in the top drawer, shutting it just as I hear the first step of the stairs creak under my nan's weight. I leap across the room and scoot under the sheets, trying to look engrossed in my book so she'll just leave the hot chocolate and go. I've just picked the book up as the door opens.

"Here you go, love. I'll just pop it here. You make sure you drink it while it's nice and hot."

"Thanks," I murmur, taking a sip. "Night." I don't look up from my book as I place the mug back down, hoping that she'll get the hint and leave, but she just stands there, hands on her hips as she looks round the room.

"Where's the...?"

I cut her off by yawning loudly, and slamming my book shut, the bang like a thunderclap in the small room. "I'm so tired. Sorry, I'm not sure what's come over me. I'd better just switch the light off and go to sleep. Night."

I put the book on the bedside table and reach for the light, switching it off, leaving the room deep in shadows except for the wedge of light that crept in from the landing.

"Shall I leave the door open a smidge? For the light?"

"No thanks, Nan, shut it too. I never sleep well if there's a door open."

"Alright then, love, night. Hope the bed bugs don't bite."

I wait until I hear the bottom step creak before I pick up my phone and set the alarm for five, resting it atop the stamped envelope that lies on the bedside table.

Once I hear the kettle whistle, I sneak across the room and wedge the chair beneath the handle to stop anyone sneaking in again while I sleep.

Slate grey light creeps round the curtains as I awake, my hand grabbing at my phone to silence the incessant chirping of my alarm. I lie there for a moment, listening to hear if it has woken Nan, hoping that if it did she'll put the sound down to the dawn chorus and go back to sleep. But the house remains quiet. I sit up and stretch, unused to being awake so early. But I want to sneak out of the house whilst Nan is still asleep, so she won't see the doll when I stuff it in the bin by the post box.

Cringing as the bed springs creak under my weight, I get up, pausing and listening between each step in case my furtive movements disturb my nan. I dress quickly then slide open the top drawer of the dresser. I choke back a cry of dismay – the drawer is empty. I slide open the other drawers, checking that I hadn't tucked the doll away between my jumpers and bras, but they hold nothing more than the clothes that I'd brought with me from home. I ease each drawer out of the chest, upending them onto the bed, before checking in the cavity behind, in case I'd thrust the doll in too hard yesterday and it had tumbled into the void behind the drawers. But other than dust and an odd sock there's nothing there. I slide each drawer back, and although I'm sure there's nothing there, I pick each item of clothing up by my fingertips, shaking it gently as if I'd seen a spider crawl between the folds of fabric, before placing it back in the drawers.

Once the last piece of clothing is back in the drawers, I shiver. Fear and tiredness sweep across my body, chilling me. Although fully dressed, I pull back the covers to crawl back into bed. I pause and stare suspiciously at the mug of half-drunk bitter chocolate that stands congealing on the bedside table, wondering if Nan had drugged me, maybe stuck a sleeping pill in it, before sneaking into my room to move the doll. It seems unlikely though, even if she knew where I'd hidden it; the chair remains wedged under the door.

I climb back into the bed, wriggling down under the covers, my jeans rucking up under my calves as I try to get comfortable. I ease one foot up to smooth out the heavy material that digs into the muscle, but instead of the feel of my sock against the bare skin of my ankle, there's a coldness, a sharp hardness that presses against my flesh. Biting back a scream I rip the covers back, drawing my legs up to my chest and flipping onto my knees in one smooth movement. There, tucked in at the bottom of the bed – its arms reaching, its legs bent as if ready to pounce – lies the doll.

Uncaring of any noise I make, I jump out of bed, already downstairs and halfway out of the front door, doll held at arm's length in a vice-like grip, before I hear the querying voice of my nan echoing down the stairs.

I strip off and jump in the shower as soon as I get back, shouting nothing more than an excuse that I'd been for a run to explain my early start and my dishevelled, sweaty appearance. The hot water feels good as it sluices away the sheen of perspiration from my skin. I scrub the hand that had shoved the doll down deep into the dumpster behind the supermarket until it's red. The skin on my fingertips puckers and bloats like a corpse's as I let the water run over it in a waterfall, trying to wash the slimy feel of the doll from my skin. It's not until the water runs cold and raises goosebumps along my already chilled skin that I step out to dry myself. Wrapping my body in the too-small, too-rough towels that lie stacked in the airing cupboard, I make my way across the landing.

The smell of bacon wafting up the stairs causes my stomach to rumble, betraying a hunger that has lain dormant under the fear and nausea that have engulfed me since my arrival. For once, with the sound of my nan singing along to the radio and the clatter of cutlery on plates, I feel good. Maybe it's not too late to rebuild what I'd lost as a child. It might be different, but that was to be expected. It wasn't as if she could be held accountable for her son's actions, in the same way that I wasn't to blame for my father's.

I hum along to the song that echoes up the stairs as I push open the bedroom door. My stomach growls at the thought of actual food after going so long without anything of substance. But my hunger dissipates as the door swings open, the stench of aftershave hitting me like tear gas. I bend over and dry heave, bile speckling the carpet between my feet.

I try to resist, but it seems as if my last ounce of strength is now splattered across the carpet. The acrid stench of vomit and bleach underlie the base scent of aftershave that permeates every inch of my room, including the sheets that my nan pulls up round my neck.

Reaching across, she pops the doll in between them, placing its head on the pillow next to mine, before smoothing the sheets and tucking them in tightly along the side of the bed, as if I was a child afraid that the monsters would grab my legs if there was an inch left loose.

"How did you...?" My voice breaks in my acid-burnt throat, the words little more than a cracked whisper. "I mean, where did you get him from? Did you make two?"

"Two what dear?"

"Two dolls." The words cause me to cough, my body spasming between the covers. The too-tight sheets digging into my throat as my body bucks.

"Why would I make two dolls dear? One is plenty."

I open my mouth to speak, but my nan lays her cool hand against my brow, her skin loose and flabby against my face. The sensation of her skin on mine causes my gorge to rise once more. I turn my head away so as not to choke on the bile in my throat, but nothing comes up, not even phlegm. The acid lies burning in my throat, choking me as I cough, tasting copper.

"Now, don't try to speak. Take a couple of deep breaths and try to get some sleep, you'll feel better soon."

A straw is lifted to my lips and I latch on, sucking deep to take away the sour taste of blood and bile. But instead of the coolness of water, the drink tastes bitter. I pull away, grimacing. Nan coos and holds my head still as she probes my mouth with the straw once more.

"Now, I know it doesn't taste nice, but you've not eaten for days, and you've thrown up anything you've drunk. So I need you to take a big sip. Come on now. It's nothing more than salts and sugars. It'll do you good."

The straw cuts against my gums as she forces it back between my lips. I steel myself and take another sip, fighting against my gag reflex as the foul taste coats my mouth, before shaking my head, the straw falling away. She looks at the half-full glass, then back at me, her eyes flicking between my face and the space next to me where the doll lies nestled under the covers. I want to turn my head, to see, to know what she's looking at, what *she's* seeing, but my body feels leaden. The weight of the blankets pressing me down into the mattress; my head heavy as it sinks into the pillow, too heavy for me to turn or lift. Even my eyelids are too heavy to keep open. Nan smiles as I drift off, her voice echoing in my head, her words obscured by the fog that drifts through me, a cloud that envelops me as I drifted further into darkness. "Yes, I think she's drunk enough."

The room is dark when I wake. I have no idea how long I've been there. The sheets hold me tight, but they no longer feel comforting; they feel like restraints, as if I was in an asylum tied to my bed. The sheets are hot and fetid as they lie stuck to my sweat-soaked skin. Panic rips through me as I realise that I'm naked. I try to remember if my nan had put me to bed like this. I never sleep naked, don't even like to wear something as skimpy as a nightie or shorts in bed, preferring the comfort of pyjamas even in the height of summer. Friends at sleepovers call me cold-blooded or frigid. But my mum has never suggested that I wear something different, even in summer when I sleep with the windows wide open and the fan on max.

I fight against the sheets, but my limbs are unresponsive; my muscles feel weak, as if made of jelly. I try to call out but my voice is little more than a whisper, either burnt away by my vomit or locked away in the same place that my limbs seem to be. My eyes dart round the dark room, the shadows forming themselves into familiar surroundings: the wardrobe, the chest of drawers, the window. Beside me I feel something shift in the bed. I try to look but my head remains stuck fast to the pillow, my eyes unable to see what the weight is that's slowly causing the aged bedsprings to sag. By the time my body has rolled into the dip that the weight had formed in the centre of the bed, whatever it is has burrowed under the covers, loosening them. Its movements cause them to billow, rising and falling in time to my chest as my breath comes fast in fear. I can feel the touch of its suit, the leather of its skin caressing mine, before I feel the ice of its lips pressed against my breast.

"Did you have fun?" My mum grabs my bags from the hallway.

"Oh, don't worry about her, she's been a bit peaky the last few days. Probably too many sweets. I've been spoiling her. Haven't I, sweetie?"

I don't flinch from my nan's touch. I've become used to it after having her bathe me; sponging my skin clean before she stripped the sheets from the bed, replacing them with ones that smelt of lavender and lotus blossom, rather than the stale stench of sweat and semen and aftershave that lay in a funk across the enclosed room.

"Shall I help you to the car with the bags?"

"Oh, that's okay we can manage. I'm glad you both had a good time. We'll have to arrange another visit soon. Come on, let's get you in the car if you're feeling peaky."

I lug the suitcase down the driveway and slide it into the back seat before getting in the front and buckling the belt, securing it over the rag doll that lies slumped on my lap. I watch as Mum slams the boot shut, and wave bye to my nan. I sit motionless, as we pull away.

"That doll's nice. Did your nan make it for you? It's a bit of an odd gift for a teenager, but I suppose she hasn't seen you since she was little. She probably still sees you as a little girl, rather than the young woman you are. I hope you weren't rude when she gave it to you."

I shake my head.

"Pity about the face. I suppose her sewing wasn't up to giving it proper features. It gives me the creeps if I'm honest, but still, I suppose the thought's there. What's it made out of?"

Her hand reaches across as if to pluck it from my lap, but I pull it away, so her fingers just dance across the sleeve of the doll's jacket. "An old suit. One of my dad's."

My mum snatches her fingers away quick, wiping them on her skirt in disgust. "Why the hell did she do that? Well, once we're home we can stick it in a cupboard somewhere out of the way. Or chuck it in the bin if you'd prefer."

My hands grip the doll tightly, drawing it back against my body, "No!" I shake my head, tears pricking at my eyes. "You can't do that. She gave it to me, it's her gift, their gift to me. You can't take it away again. It reminds me of my dad."

|Acknowledgements|

∿

There are so many people to thank for this book. First of all I must thank Steve Shaw for all his hard work and in agreeing to publish this odd little collection. I must also thank him again for being an awesome friend, here's to many more games of crazy golf.

My thanks also go to James Worrad whose wonderful artwork graces the covers of this collection, you sir are a scholar and a gent (sorry I was mixing you up with someone else, but I do owe your Awesomeness a pint the next time I see you).

My thanks go out to all those editors and publishers that have taken a chance on me and my writing, a special thanks must go to Adele Wearing, Justin Parks, Tracy Fahey, Theresa Derwin, Steve Shaw (again), Phil Sloman, Peter Mark May, Sophie Essex, Lee Murray and Marie O'Regan.

It takes a writing community to publish a book, there are so many people behind the scenes and I must thank all those who have beta read my stories. So shout-outs to Tabatha Wood, Charlotte Bond, Priya Sharma, Tracy Fahey and Gary Couzens, all of whom have had to deal with my run on sentences and love of the comma.

Although I have forsaken them for the sunny south coast, I must also thank the wonderful writing community of the East Midlands, especially Katie Sone, Farhana Shaikh, Alex Davis and Pixie Peigh.

To say I was ecstatic to have Robert Shearman agree to write my introduction to this collection would be an understatement (or hyperbole, I always get those two mixed up). I have always loved his short stories and was as giddy as a school girl when I first met him. Thank you for agreeing to write the introduction, and thank you for being a wonderful friend. Sorry again for all those times I managed to accidentally insult you, it was nothing but nerves.

Finally I must thank my ever suffering husband Simon, who drowns out my whinging about writing by dreaming of launch wine.

CPSIA information can be obtained
at www.ICGtesting.com
Printed in the USA
BVHW071327300922
648381BV00003B/68

9 781913 038793